cop. 2

JF   Wallin, Luke
          The slavery ghosts

The Slavery Ghosts

The Slavery Ghosts

by Luke Wallin

BRADBURY PRESS   SCARSDALE, NEW YORK

Bradbury Press, Inc.
2 Overhill Road, Scarsdale, NY 10583
An affiliate of Macmillan, Inc.
Collier Macmillan Canada, Inc.
The text of this book is set in 11 pt. Galliard.
Manufactured in the United States of America
1 3 5 7 9 10 8 6 4 2
Library of Congress Cataloging in Publication Data
Wallin, Luke.
The slavery ghosts.
Summary: Two children, convinced by a "visitation," aid the escape of a
child's spirit, trapped for more than one hundred years in the tunnels be-
neath a historic Southern mansion.
[1. Ghosts—Fiction] I. Title.
PZ7.W15934Sl   1983   [Fic]   83-2679
ISBN 0-02-792380-0

For Jake and Livy,
Phil, Enid, and Cass

And their parents
Tom and Sue

CHAPTER ONE

An Unpleasant Footstep

Number One Wisteria Road was the address of the old
house, and its name was Tapalyla Hill. Even though one
could no longer stand on its grand second-floor balcony
and see the Tapalyla River at sunset—a curving ribbon
of bright copper in the pines—at least the mansion was
still surrounded on the lower slopes with its own tall
trees. The river had been straightened by the govern-
ment, and its new banks were lined with giant electrical
and neon signs, for pizza, game rooms, discos and
Skateland, blocking the balcony's vision of what was now
muddy canal water. Yet Tapalyla Hill was as elegant as
it had been on the day it was completed, in 1850. Huge
pines and oaks graced the lower terraces, and each trunk
was wound around by gnarled and ancient vines of wisteria, sending their tentacles to the very tops of the tim-
ber, and at a certain moment in spring covering the
whole forested scene with the sugary sweet aroma of
their wine-colored blossoms.

It was a fitting place for a ghost to live.

For just as the house remained intact and cloaked with its own sense of enchantment, so its ghost story was repeated with more conviction than any others in town. The hill beneath the mansion was supposed to be a maze of tunnels or caves, secret passages connecting with others from similar houses, leading finally to the high bank of the river.

When the Yankee troops invaded, all the wealthy ladies and gentlemen had expected to enter the caves, walk quickly through the earth—tunneled out by their slaves—and escape to a riverboat, which would carry them faster than the current to Mobile, on the Gulf of Mexico.

The tunnels were never used, except as nameless grave sites for the slaves who died during the rushed and miserable work. It was said their bones still lay exposed in the sealed-off caves, and that their ghosts stalked the dark and unmapped passageways.

But they weren't the only unhappy and roaming spirits on the hill. Tapalyla Hill was said to be inhabited by the tragic Mrs. Ruffin, wife of the Confederate colonel who had once owned the place. In each generation since the Civil War except for the present one, her wispy and moaning form had been spotted about the house. But it was all a matter of waiting, according to Granny Blake, who kept the legend of Mrs. Ruffin alive and well. "I will see her any time now," Granny often said.

Granny lived at Tapalyla Hill with her daughter, Amy, and her family. Amy was a pretty woman of thirty-three, who felt she had barely survived being raised as a Southern Belle. Amy's husband, Dr. Maynard James, was a man as fiercely proud of the Old South as his mother-in-law, with whom he agreed on little else. When Amy married Maynard, and he began making all his "big doctor money," as Granny also said, she had suggested he restore the mansion so they could all live there together. But he wouldn't do it. He made her deed half of it over to his wife before he poured his thousands upon thousands into making the house "shine and glow," as Amy described it, mocking the whole thing.

Their children were Jake, thirteen, and Livy, twelve. As things turned out, they would be the first to see the mansion's true ghost, and to discover the reason for the long and restless haunting.

Livy stood with Jake in the shadow of a two-hundred-year-old magnolia tree and surveyed their house. It should have been a tranquil sight, with spring upon them, sweet winey wisteria scent on the soft air, and bees flying drunkenly among the bright white-flowered dogwoods and the neat rows of pink and purple azaleas. But the place seemed to pulse and breathe with an angry presence they had never felt before.

"I promise you," Jake said, "that I'm not making it up. Not a single word of it."

Livy turned on one foot, gazing off into the honeysuckle, avoiding his face, wanting not to choose. She hadn't admitted she felt the presences in his room, too; she didn't want to encourage his fear.

"So make up your mind right now," Jake said. "Either you believe me, and you're with me, or you aren't."

Livy kicked a root, and watched a doodlebug curl up into a gray ball, its ridiculous version of playing possum.

"Yes or no," Jake continued. "I need you, Liv, to figure this thing out. And I can't be spending my time convincing you the noises really exist."

She was on the spot, pinned. "Oh all right," she said slowly.

"Don't say it if you don't mean it with all your heart."

She raised one eyebrow and peeked at him with the brown eye beneath it. "With all my heart?"

He blushed. "Aw, Livy, you know what I mean."

"I said okay, didn't I? I guess I believe you. No. I do."

He looked frustrated.

"Really," she added.

"I'll take it," Jake said. "I'll believe you trust me. Because it's driving me crazy that they won't."

"I'll bet."

"It's so unfair—you'd think at least Mom would believe me. *Boy!* She's lived here all her life."

"I know," Livy said sympathetically.

"She would believe me, if she just weren't so busy. But when she comes home tired and all, and I say maybe there's a ghost in the attic, she thinks I'm a crackpot."

Livy felt herself being drawn deeper into Jake's predicament.

"You might think," she said, "that Granny would be the one to take this seriously."

"Granny!" Jake said, rolling his eyes.

"I mean," Livy continued, "she's always claimed the ghost of Mrs. Ruffin lives in our house."

"But don't forget who's supposed to see it first."

"Yeah."

"She's really going out of her way to make fun of me."

"She laughed at you in front of Mom and Daddy at supper."

Jake nodded.

"That made me so mad," Livy said. "I hate her sometimes."

"You're not supposed to say that."

"I don't care," Livy said, holding her chin up at the house and Granny inside.

"Jesus doesn't want us to hate."

"I can't help it!"

"I know why you're so mad at her," Jake said. "Because she wants you to be in the Old Confederacy Celebration, and you haven't told her you won't . . . I remember how cute you were last year, you little Celebration Belle."

"You shut up, Jake. Just leave me alone."

"Livy, don't get mad at me. I agree with you; I don't want you to be in the stupid thing."

"Stop teasing me, then." She took a breath, sighed deeply, and turned away from him. "It's so idiotic," she said. "Dressing up like a little cutie pie for a bunch of strangers to stare at."

"That's what you think now," Jake said, "because Mom said the same thing. But you and Mom and I are the only ones in this whole town who think that way. All your friends will be in it."

Livy leaned against the tree trunk and closed her eyes. "I know," she said.

"And during the Great Depression, when Granny lived here and it was run down, she made part of her living from those tourists."

"Don't start lecturing me, Jake James. I've heard that a thousand times. Granny survived the Great Depression; that's why she sucks the goodness out of fried chicken necks; that's why she doesn't need to attend picture shows. I know all about it."

"Okay," he said, laughing softly, "you're just so much fun to tease."

"You, too," she said, looking up at the house. Jake stopped laughing.

"Let's go up to my room," he said, "and see what we hear. Please, Livy!"

She made him wait a long time, so he would appreciate her company, and finally she turned to him.

"Let's go," she said sweetly.

They crossed the garden and entered the mansion, which, as always, felt as though it were alive. They weren't sure why—could it be because Granny and her friends always talked about the antebellum houses as if they were living beings? Or did the places actually feel that way, each with its own character and closely held secret past? Now the past felt nearer than it ever had before.

They reached Jake's room on the second floor and opened the door.

Three days ago when the heavy footsteps across the ceiling started, Jake had gone to the attic to look around. When nothing turned up and the crunching continued he had called in his parents to listen. But they never heard anything, and after the third of these episodes they lost patience with him, and told him to thump back.

When he tried this with a broom handle, just an hour earlier, there was an angry-seeming stomp on the ceiling, and he had run for the garden where Livy had found him.

Now they stood in his room again, waiting.

"Try the broom," she said.

He nodded. Then he raised it and tapped once, waited, tried again, then three times.

Livy sighed and looked at him.

There was a slow, deep-sounding step above them, and the long creaking of a dry attic beam.

Jake and Livy watched each other's eyes widen, and felt chillbumps on their arms and necks.

"It's true!" she whispered. "Try it again!"

He raised it to tap, but just before the broom handle reached the plaster the loud crunch was repeated.

"Somebody's up there," Livy said with a tremor in her voice.

"That's what I've been trying to tell everybody."

"It doesn't sound like a ghost," Livy said in a loud whisper.

"Oh, really? What does it sound like, then?"

"A great big man," she replied. "Somebody I don't want to meet."

"Yeah."

"Shall we find Granny, and all of us have a look?"

"All of us?"

"Granny first," she said.

They laughed nervously and jumped at the excuse to get out of the room and close the door. In the hallway Jake said, "We can try, but I know what will happen."

"Whoever that is can't get away," Livy said. "The attic steps are shut up."

"You think it's a flesh-and-blood person, don't you?"

"Well, maybe."

Jake flushed with anger.

"All right, I'm going to prove it to you. Stay right here and watch the steps, so you'll know he's still up there, and I'll go ask Granny to come."

"That's okay," Livy said. "I'll go with you."

They found Granny in the kitchen, directing two of her friends as well as their borrowed maids in a spirited cleaning operation.

"You don't know what these tourists will do!" Granny was saying. "They pretend to be listening to me, and all the while they're running their fingers along under the counter tops, or the tables, checking for dust. Don't you laugh!" she shrieked at one of her friends. "If they ever once came to your house, you'd know."

"Granny?" Livy asked.

Granny spun quickly and gracefully around.

"Livy! Child, I've been hunting you all day. Where have you been?"

Jake snickered.

"Hiding!" Granny said, hearing him. "Avoiding your heritage!"

"Granny," Livy said, "we have to ask you something."

"Don't try to distract me, Miss Livy. This house is preparing itself for the Celebration, and it needs all our help. You are disappointing this house and all who live here."

"Granny," Jake said, "could we speak with you in the other room, please ma'am?"

He said this in his most courtly, gentlemanly voice, which sometimes worked with her.

As soon as they were alone Jake explained about the footsteps in the attic.

"So," he concluded, "since Mom and Daddy don't believe me, I came to you. Maybe it's the ghost of Mrs. Ruffin?"

She cocked a shrewd eye, thinking it over. She knew the children wouldn't turn to her about anything if they had a choice. And just possibly this was some kind of a trick, like the time they hid her favorite pillow in the garage and let it mildew before they gave it back.

"I have no time for pranks," she said, "but it won't take long to clear this up. Open the attic, young man."

"Yes, ma'am," Jake said, running for the hall.

He caught the hanging rope and pulled down the folded steps. When they were locked in place, making a stairway, he stepped aside and bowed, letting Granny go first.

She smiled politely at his bow, another old southern gesture that never failed to make her happy, and she put her foot onto the first step. Her long arm went out to the wall switch, and the attic hole lit up.

She quickly mounted the stairs, poking her beauty-parlor hair, a stiff blue-gray fluffed ball, up into the space.

The children knew it was very hot there, and the search would all be over when she felt the first drop glistening, as she said, on her forehead.

"Helloooooooo!" Granny called out, challenging any and all.

There was no response.

She turned to and fro, gave the children one hard glance and rapped the attic floor with her sharp, bony knuckles. Jake thought about how those quick knobs felt administered to his head when he used a forbidden word, like calling a baby a kid, or saying "ain't."

"She's up there, Granny!" Livy cried. "I heard her, too!"

Granny hesitated a second, then climbed on into the attic. They listened as she crossed the space several times, looking behind boxes of old clothes, giant stacks of *National Geographic*s and her trunks of authentic Confederate uniforms and swords.

Then she backed rapidly down the steps.

When she turned to face the children her severe, thin face was dotted with beads of water, and her blue eyes were fierce. She touched the springy edge of her hair.

"No, she's not," Granny said with a level anger that kept them from speaking. "Jake, replace the steps. This minute."

"Yes, ma'am," he said sadly. Not only hadn't they encountered the ghost, but now they had a hot mad granny on their hands.

"And Miss Livy, I'm so glad you found me, since I

couldn't locate you all day long. I have something to say."

Livy's eyes drifted to the window.

"Are you listening to me?"

"Yes 'um."

"Very well. You don't want to be in the Old Confederacy Celebration. Heavens, child, if I got everything I wanted do you think I'd spend my time maintaining our heritage for a bunch of Yankees and Texans who have the money to travel?"

"I thought you loved it," Jake blurted out.

"Hush, young man! I'm talking to your sister right now. Your daddy has been chosen General of the Ball this year—the honor of a lifetime. This is not a question of pleasure. This is not a matter of want to and don't want to. This is your *duty*, girl."

Now she was bearing down with all her personal force on Livy, whose lip was trembling.

"You are not your own person, Miss Livy, as you seem to think. You are the raw material of this family. You are the blank page upon which it is my duty to write! For you to refuse service in the Celebration is as if Jake grew up to become a draft dodger!"

"Granny . . ." Livy said. Jake thought she was about to break down and cry, and maybe give in. He wondered if he would surrender under Granny's treatment.

But Livy's eyes narrowed now, as she returned Granny's stare, and her lip was still.

"Go write on someone else's page!" Livy said, and she took off on a run.

"Come back here!" Granny cried, drawing herself up to her full, modest height.

"Wait till I tell your mother!" she said. And then, slumping a little, she muttered, "Your mother. She's *responsible* for this complete lack of pride!"

CHAPTER TWO

A Voice From Beyond

Jake caught up with Livy in the garden.

"I can't stand it in this house any more," she said. "I mean it."

"Aw, Liv."

He walked along beside her, and she led the way across the street and down the sidewalk.

"Really, Jake, Granny's driving me crazy."

"I know."

"No, you don't. You get to wear pants every day; nobody wants *you* to put on long dresses with ruffles!"

He chuckled.

"I might just run away," Livy said.

"Oh, yeah? Listen: I might, too, if those noises in my room don't stop."

"I wouldn't blame you," she said angrily, walking a little faster.

Jake wondered where she was headed. But he didn't question Livy's seriousness—she made up her mind quickly about things; in fact, he wished he could be as decisive as she was.

"What do you think's up there?" he asked.

"What or who?"

"You really think it's a person?"

"It could be—remember that nut in Memphis who lived in church attics?"

"Oh, yeah. He kidnapped a little girl and kept her with him for four months."

"Don't talk about it," she said with a shudder.

"He didn't hurt her, though. It seemed he just wanted a Scrabble partner, remember?"

"It seems he got away, too, Jake. The maniac is still loose."

"True. But Memphis is a long way from here."

"Jake," she said with a sharp glance, "my point is . . . it could be *another* nut."

"Oh. In our attic?"

She stopped, hands on hips, and sighed. "What else were we talking about?"

"I just hadn't thought about it being alive . . . with a body and all."

Livy set out walking with long strides again.

"Say," Jake said, running to catch up, "where are we going anyway?"

"I'm deciding some things."

"I know that, but where are we—"

"For a Popsicle," she said. "Do you want one?"

"Sure." He grinned.

"I'm buying."

"Great. Big spender, huh?"

"If I decide to leave home," Livy said, "I'll need some favors from you."

"Oh."

He wanted to get her mind off that idea, so he brought up his problem again, and the new fear she'd mentioned—that a crazy kidnapping lunatic might be in their attic.

"Either way," Jake said, "whether it's a ghost or a nut, I'm in trouble."

"I wouldn't sleep in there, if I were you," Livy advised.

"I guess you're right," he said. Why, he wondered, did Livy seem to think of the good ideas first, just a second before he was about to?

They picked out purple Popsicles, and stood in front of the little store taking a few licks. Jake was relieved when Livy started out slowly in the direction of home.

"Have you decided to stay?" he asked.

She scowled at him. "For the time being. I won't leave you with this ghost thing."

"You won't? Thanks."

It occurred to Jake how much scarier this would be without Livy's spirit on his side.

They walked on, and the warm air drifted over their Popsicles, which were melting fast. A honeybee circled around and around Livy's.

"Get away!" she said, flicking her wrist at it.

The last piece of her Popsicle went flying.

"Oh, no," she sighed.

"Too bad," Jake said quickly, unable to resist a teasing tone of voice.

She looked angrily at him, and he saw that her brown eyes were watery and her cheeks flushed. She walked rapidly away from him, almost running.

"Wait!" he said. "I'm sorry. Really! Here, I'll share mine."

"You will?"

"Uh-huh," he groaned, catching up with her and handing it over.

She took a few big licks, showing her purple tongue, and handed it back.

A few steps later a honeybee found Jake.

"Get back!" he cried.

Then the bee's friends and family discovered the party, and they began to pour out of a crape myrtle and whine excitedly all around Jake.

"No!" he screamed. "Leave me alone!"

He was determined not to lose his Popsicle as Livy had, and he covered it with his free hand. But the bees were spinning around him, brushing his neck and ears, and juice was dipping on his tennis shoes, which had been white.

"Throw that thing down, child!" a strong female voice said.

He flung it into the crape myrtle, and the bees swung into wide, confused arcs, then followed it out of sight.

"That was awful," Livy said. "They must have a hive near here."

"Yeah." Jake smiled. "Why did you call me 'child'?" he asked.

"I didn't call you anything."

"Didn't you say, 'Throw that thing down, child!'?"

"I thought it, for sure. But I didn't say a word."

Jake's eyebrows moved toward his eyes, and his lips went together as if he had tasted a green persimmon.

"What's worrying you?" Livy asked.

"Somebody warned me," he said. "Some woman."

"Maybe you just read my mind."

"No—it was loud!"

Livy shrugged her shoulders. "Maybe those ghosts have infected your brain," she said sarcastically.

"That's just great, Liv. Be silly about it."

"Jake, ghosts in the attic are one thing, but inside your *mind?*"

He walked away angrily.

When they reached the big house their father was standing in the driveway loading his pickup.

"Hey, Jake boy!" he said, tossing in a portable blind of camouflage cloth.

"Hi, Daddy."

"Hi," Livy said.

"Oh, hi, Liv. Jake, tomorrow morning is you know what."

"Turkey season."

"Ummm-hummmmm!" He smiled with his eyes closed. "And I know where the biggest gobbler on the whole club is roosting. Want to come with me?"

"Uh, when are you going?"

"I'm heading out in just a little while. Got to stop by the hospital and see a few folks, then I'm going to the clubhouse to spend the night."

Jake felt a hard pinch on his arm and jumped.

Livy was giving him a sharp look. She whispered in his ear, "You're *not* leaving me here with Granny!"

Jake still felt angry with Livy. Was she on his side or not?

"Or with those footsteps!" she added.

Jake turned toward his father. "I'm sorry, Daddy, but I can't. I have something I've got to do."

His father shook his head once to the side. It meant he was mighty disappointed. He pulled his truck seat forward and laid his shotgun in its case behind it.

"Maybe I can go next week," Jake said.

"Hope so," his father said, not looking at him, restlessly checking over his equipment.

"If he goes, I'm going," Livy said.

Her father cocked an eyebrow and smiled at her.

"Now I've heard it all," he said, jumping into the pickup cab.

He slammed the door and cranked up.

"Y'all be good now," he said, backing down the long drive.

When he was out of sight they still stood looking after him.

"He thinks only boys should hunt," Livy said.

"I don't even want to."

"I don't either. I think it's terrible—to make a noise like a nice hen bird, and make the gobbler come running . . ."

"And then blow his head off," Jake said.

"That's right."

"Well, why did you ask Daddy if you could go?"

"Just to tease him," she said, tossing her hair back.

Livy led the way into the garden.

"Know what Granny said?" she asked.

"Who cares?" Jake said.

"She said all Daddy's friends have little boys who like to hunt turkeys with them."

"So *what?*"

"Granny thinks that makes you weird."

"I think they're weird."

"Granny said you're afraid to shoot the shotgun."

"Oh, yeah? Well I haven't seen her blasting away with any shotguns lately, have you?"

"No," Livy said, laughing.

Jake turned away. Did Daddy think he was afraid of the shotgun? Is that where Granny got the idea?

They began to climb the largest magnolia tree, with its huge low arms like benches in the air.

It's true, Jake thought, I hate the loudness of it, and the kick. I hate it! He wished he could do something really brave, once and for all, and prove to himself and everybody else the kind of boy he was. Or wished he was.

Dusk was beginning to fall over the garden and the house. They heard the soft calling of a barred owl in the distance and, closer by, hidden in the hedges, the trilling of doves. When the magnolia shadows began to grow darker, the windows of the great house were lit with yellow lamplight. And above them in the lavender sky bullbats streaked and darted.

In the silence Jake wondered about the noises in his room, and tried to decide where he might sleep without angering his parents.

Livy was thinking about how busy Daddy always was, either tending to his patients or his hunting. She remembered a few nice times when the whole family had sat around a fire in the evening together, reading and talking, but not very many. When Mom suggested a fire, Daddy usually said they were too much trouble, and anyway he had to run out for a late-night check on the intensive care ward, or to see a friend about a hound dog, or a jeep, or a membership in a new hunting club. Restless and rich, was how Granny described him.

Suddenly Livy saw something materializing in the air before them. Jake felt her hand on his knee, and the grip was tight.

"Jake!" she said in a strained whisper.

"Huh?"

Then he saw it, too—a form, woman-sized, floating just over the path, a few feet away. It was like a large black woman, beginning to take definite shape out of a cloud of fog, and partaking of the shadows, too. Jake was rigid.

"Who are you?" he said. But his voice hardly worked better than Livy's.

"My name Sarantha," the form said. "An' stop bein' afraid. Right now."

"Yes, ma'am," Jake said.

He recognized that voice.

CHAPTER THREE

Secret Knowledge

Jake and Livy slid closer together on the low limb until their jeans were touching. Her hand was still locked like a claw on his kneecap.

"That was *me* told you to get back from them bees, don't you remember?"

"Un-huh," Jake said.

"You wouldn't be no good to me all stung up. Thas why I been watchin' after you."

"You have? Are you a—?" Jake's voice became wispy and then vanished altogether.

"A ghost?" the form said.

"Yes, ma'am," Livy whispered.

"I suppose thas what you all would call me," Sarantha said sadly. "But of course I don't call *myself* that!"

"You don't?" Livy asked. Jake was amazed that her voice sounded normal.

"No, child! I'm a livin' spirit, jus' like you."

"Oh."

"Was that you in my room?" Jake managed.

"Them noises on yo' ceiling?"

"Yes, ma'am."

"I reckon not! I don't go around scarin' folks, if I can help it."

"You're scaring me," Livy said.

"No, I'm not!" Sarantha said ominously, coming a little closer.

"Okay, okay," Livy said, holding up a palm.

"Them things in yo' attic," Sarantha said to Jake, "are some of the worst spirits I have had the bad luck to come across, in all my travels."

"In all your travels," Jake said with a swallow, trying to imagine what travels she had known.

"Thas right," Sarantha said, seeming to warm up a little. "All them spirits in yo' attic are here for the Old Confederacy Celebration. See, they is the evilest of the evil, the vilest of the vile. They's like the Ku Klux Klan of the spirit world."

"Yuck," Livy said. "I don't want them in *my* house."

"Bless you, child. They won't stay long. All the white folks celebratin' the old slavery days is what called 'em up. They hopin' to meet their leader, an' start on the rampage."

"The Celebration called them up?" Jake said.

"Thas it. All that hot energy, concentrated right on Tapalyla Hill, yo' house."

"Granny's energy," Livy said.

"She a sight, yo' granny," Sarantha said. "She ain't got a bad heart, like them ghosts, but she misguided, sho' is."

"Where is their leader?" Jake asked.

"Well, thas the part of the story that breaks my heart, honey. He locked in a place called the below-world, with my darlin' little daughter Darcy. They been beyond the timegate since the Civil War, mo' than a hundred years ago. Ever since they done agreed to it."

"Agreed to what?" Livy asked.

"See, once upon a bad bad time we was all slaves, me an' Darcy, an' our friend William an' a whole bunch of good folks; we belonged to Colonel Ruffin, an' he used to own yo' house, too."

"Colonel Ruffin!" Jake said. "His wife is supposed to haunt Tapalyla Hill! Granny says—"

"Hold on," Sarantha interrupted. "I knows all about what yo' granny says. But Miz Ruffin was one of the very few white peoples livin' in slavery times who stood up against it. She helped mo' than one black soul escape on the underground railroad; you ever heard of that?"

"Mom told us," Livy said.

"Thas good. Some little southern white children never heard nothin' about it yet. Anyway, Miz Ruffin been free of slavery ever since; her spirit dealin' with higher things, you could say, an' she doin' jus' fine. But now the colonel . . . He rotten as he used to be, sho' is."

"He's still alive?" Jake said. "Is that him in the attic?"

"If y'all would hush an' let me talk, I would try explainin' some things."

"Sorry," Livy said.

"Well, Colonel Ruffin was a mean man, an' he used to beat us fo' no reason anybody knew of. When the war was finally over, that man jus' couldn't take it in.

He wouldn't believe it. An' he tried to go right on livin' like he had befo'."

"But he couldn't, right?" Livy asked, caught up in the story.

"We all run off in the night," Sarantha said, "an' he come chasin' us on his horse. He caught us out in the big pasture, underneath the moon, and he commenced to shootin' an' killin'."

"Oh, no," Livy said.

Sarantha held up her hand.

"I was the first to die," she said. "Then a few mo' fell. The res' he herded back to the plantation like a flock of sheep, an' locked 'em down in the basement. He tol' William and Darcy they could live free of them cellar cages if they would be his personal house servants; otherwise, he gon' lock them up, too."

"How horrible," Livy said.

"This was in our house?" Jake asked.

"Un-huh. Now, here's what happened. William and Darcy promised the po' souls in the cages they would come an' release them one night. Then they pretended to go 'long with Colonel Ruffin, an' be his good servants."

"But they saved the others?" Livy said excitedly.

"Sho' did not. They broke they's word, both of 'em did. William, he continued as the master's servant. Darcy, she run off to the swamp. Them old friends of theirs, they laid in them cellar pens till they clothes rotted off."

"*Euuuuuu,*" Livy said.

"See, Darcy was too scared to keep her promise, an'

so was old William. Both of 'em got sick from the guilt of it, from thinkin' of their friends, an' thas how they died: free an' guilty."

"They weren't very free, were they?" Livy asked.

"You comin' to the point now, child, sho' is. The day finally come when Darcy couldn't live with herself no mo'; she had to get them slaves out of them cages, or die tryin'. She slipped up to the house an' got inside, an' made her way down the basement steps. Oh, y'all should of heard the rejoicin' then."

"So she did save them after all?" Livy asked.

"Shhhhh. My baby los' her nerve. She standin' right there with the lantern, ready to do right, an' she took shakin' till she dropped the key. It was so ringin' loud she was 'fraid to pick it up; jus' stood there starin' at it. Next thing happened, Colonel Ruffin heard the racket, an' come downstairs to check. He made William walk in front. Well, when the colonel seen Darcy, he lost what head he had. He commenced to screamin' an' slashin', an' he never quit until he finished his work, an' every one of them po' peoples lay dead on the cold stone floor."

"He murdered them all?" Jake asked.

"Sho' did. An' he was still mad, still hatin', wantin' more slashin' an' bashin', wishin' with all his heart fo' mo' slaves to kill. I'm tellin' y'all, he was sick an' mean both."

"How did he finally die?" Jake asked.

"He walked back an' forth amongst those bodies, back an' forth, cuttin' the air itself with his bloody sword, workin' himself up madder an' madder an' madder, till all at once somethin' busted loose in his heart, an' he fell down dead as the res'."

"Good!" Livy said. "At least one good thing happened!"

"Hold on," Sarantha said, slightly breathless. "It ain't as simple as that. Honey, when folks die with that much hatred, an' that much fear, sometimes they can't do nothin' but stew an' stew in the spirit world. They can't have rest, they can't move on to a new life, they can't do nothin' at all, 'cept worry an' hate, an' wish they'd lived a different life. Maybe it's a part of hell; I wouldn't be surprised."

"So those are the unhappy spirits in our attic?" Jake asked.

"No, wrong again, son. See, Colonel Ruffin an' Darcy an' the others, they all wanted so badly to relive their lives, it was all they could think about. The colonel couldn't imagine livin' any kind of way without slaves. An' the po' slaves, they wanted another chance so they could escape him, an' not die miserable an' mad. Darcy an' William, they 'specially needed a new start, to keep their promises. So in the higher and better parts of their spirits, they all entered into a special contract with one another, to spend a hundred mo' years in a ghost-place jus' like the plantation; they'd start up right where they lef' off, with Colonel Ruffin havin' slaves in his cages, an' Darcy livin' wild in the woods, 'fraid to do the rescue she promised. This way, everybody gon' have another chance. They agreed to a hundred years, an' I sho' hate to tell you what: that time is almost gone. In two mo' days the below-world be destroyed fo'ever, an' all them souls got to move on to their next lives carryin' the same old hate, fear, guilt an' sin."

"It's so sad," Livy said.

"It breaks my heart in two," Sarantha said. "If only Darcy found the courage, somewhere inside, to slip up on the big house one mo' time . . . Then she be free of all that, an' be with me again."

"But who's in our attic?" Jake asked.

"Them are some loose redneck spirits of this world," Sarantha said. "They hopin' the colonel will find the timegate befo' the below-world come to its end. If he do, he'll be up here as mean as ever, ready to lead them into mischief again—see, long time ago they was in his regiment, servin' the southern cause."

"Ohhhhh," Jake said. "Now I get it."

"Yes."

At last, Sarantha seemed out of words, and tears rolled silently down her ghostly cheeks.

"Is there any chance Darcy will still escape?" Livy asked.

"Not much of one. She know where the timegate is, but she too scared to go there. Besides, she ain't fulfilled her lifework, which is freein' the slavery ghosts in them cages."

"Can't you help her?" Jake asked.

"No, child. Can't nobody go through the timegate from this end."

"Where is it?"

"Down in the tunnel beneath yo' house."

Sarantha raised a plump, ghostly arm and pointed toward the boarded-up door under their porch.

"The cave!"

"Thas right. An' on the other side, down below, it's out in the big pasture. Now the colonel, he don't know exactly where it is; his lifework was to overcome his hate, an' let them slaves go free of his own accord. If he'd a done that, then Darcy was to lead him to the timegate. See how it could have been?"

"Wait just a second," Jake said. "Let me understand something. Your daughter and her friends and this awful colonel all agreed to this? Like a play?"

"Yes," Sarantha said sadly. "It be hard to explain; we all doin' things we planned—livin' up to the bes' part or the worst part, whether we in a flesh-an'-blood life, or one them in-between times. But the part of you that makes these deals is way beyond yo' so-called ordinary self. Jus' like you way past yo' little baby self that you used to be. Can you understand all this, honey?"

"Are you talking about reincarnation?" Livy asked.

"Sho' am, child."

"One of Mom's friends believes in that."

"Thas good."

"And you're saying we plan our lives? Even with people like Colonel Ruffin?"

"Un-huh."

"But then why don't I remember planning this life?" Jake asked.

"Thas a smart question," Sarantha said. "An' the answer's right here: if you was to remember everythin' all the time, baby talk, past lives, dreams in the night—why, you wouldn't have no life at all! Thas the whole point of dyin', to give you a chance to remember, think things over an' over, an' plan yo' next move."

"Is all this really true?" Livy asked.

"It sho' is; I knows how hard such new thoughts be."

"Then what's my lifework, right now?"

"Look deep within yo'self . . ." Sarantha said, beginning to fade away.

"Wait!" Jake cried. "We want to ask you some more!"

"I hates to think of it all," Sarantha said tearfully, "because I jus' know my Darcy's gon' fail again, an' die again when the below-world go."

"Isn't there anything we can do?" Livy asked.

"Goodbye," Sarantha said, disappearing. "I jus' wanted you to know 'bout them attic souls; they be gone soon, one way or another."

There was nothing but silence and shadows.

Jake grabbed Livy's hand, which was still clamped painfully over his knee.

"Do you mind?" he asked.

"Oh, sorry."

He slid off the tree branch and tried to put his weight on that leg, but it was asleep.

"I'm kind of in shock," he said.

"Me, too."

"Livy, nobody will ever believe us."

"I know it."

They heard the screen door slam.

"Children!" Granny shrieked. "Children?! Are you out there? If you don't come in this house right this minute I'm calling the police!"

"Good grief," Livy said.

"Come on," Jake said, hopping up and down on his good leg. "Let's go see what's eating her."

"At least we know there's a nice ghost around," she said as they walked.

"Yeah. But what about those creeps in the attic? And why are they bumping on my ceiling?"

"I don't know. But they'll be gone soon."

"And something else bothers me, Liv. When Sarantha first appeared she said something about me being of use to her."

"She did?"

"You remember—she saved me from the bees because I wouldn't be any use 'all stung up,' as she put it."

"Oh, yeah."

Livy shrugged; Jake didn't know what to make of it either. Anyway, now it was time to deal with Granny.

They walked up the steps and into the house.

"Is that you?" Granny said from the kitchen. They heard her quick footsteps coming.

"Yes," Livy sighed, "it's us."

"So I see!" she said, mouth drawn tight. "And where may I ask—"

"We went for a walk," Jake said.

"A long one," Livy added. "Where's Mom?"

"Your mother called," Granny said, "and she has to study tonight, at the university library. She will not be home until well after your bedtime."

"Oh, no," Livy said. "I need to talk to her."

"Leave the poor woman alone," Granny said, "and let her do her silly work."

"It's not silly," Jake said.

"Your father, young man, was back here, too. He's going to his hunting camp for the night. It seems that tomorrow morning is the first day of wild turkey season."

"I know that."

"He wanted to ask you to go with him, but, oh, no, you weren't anywhere to be found. However, he said if you decide you want to come, to have his answering service call him on his beeper."

"Thanks," Jake said.

"Well?" Granny said. "Are you going to call him, and make him drive all the way back to town?"

"No," Jake said quietly. "You know I don't care anything about killing a turkey. Anyway, I already spoke to him."

"Your father must be mighty disappointed in you, Jake. It's an old southern tradition—father and son, out on the first morning of the season. You ought to be ashamed."

Jake was looking at his shoe, and silently tapping his toe, as he held back his tongue.

"What's for supper?" Livy asked, hoping to come to Jake's rescue.

"You might have helped," Granny said sharply, "but as it happened one of the maids I had on loan today is a wonderful cook, and I made her stay late to fix it. Nothing much—just hot corn bread, fresh greens, fried chicken and apple pie. Nothing you'd be interested in."

"*Mmmmmm,*" Jake said, rubbing his stomach.

They washed their hands and hurried to the dining room.

Granny took the opportunity to sit at the head of the table, in their father's chair.

"Bow you heads," she said.

They did, and Granny said grace.

"Oh, Lord," she began, "we thank Thee for this meal, that Thou hast given us. We thank Thee for this day, which we have dedicated to Thy service, thank Thee for these little children, all we have to carry on the legacy of this great family, and bless them in their efforts to understand what Thou dost expect of them. In Jesus' name, amen."

Soon the children were deep into their fried chicken, and there was a great silence except for the munching.

"The house is clean," Granny said, "sparkling clean, spanking clean, clean enough for *Southern Living* magazine. And that's the way it's going to stay. Do y'all hear me?"

They nodded.

"This old woman has worked and slaved, all day long, directing help that couldn't find it's own shoelace, if you know what I mean. And, I might add, without a stitch of assistance from certain young persons."

They tried to ignore this.

"A certain number of Yankees will come here," Granny continued. "We can't keep them out. Goodness, you can't even tell who they are sometimes until they're inside your house, asking questions with those clipped-off words of theirs. There isn't anything more coldhearted than a Yankee," she said with a fierce gleam in her eyes, "and don't you ever forget it."

Jake had heard such words all his life. But Mom had told him straight out that they weren't true. He couldn't understand why something not true could be so important to Granny.

Jake and Livy were careful not to say anything that would make their grandmother angry enough to withhold their pie, so they were quiet through the meal, just politely nodding when Granny asked her questions.

"I guess it might do them good, after all," she said during the apple pie course. "Poor Yankees don't have anything like the Celebration in their lives at home. They have a crass, mean society, ruined long ago by industry and too much rushing about, trying to make money. A Yankee doesn't know what it's like to take a quiet walk in a well-kept garden. That's what they tried to take away from us, in the War."

Jake and Livy knew she meant the Civil War.

"Thanks for supper," Jake said when he finally finished the last bite of pie.

"Me, too," Livy said. "May I be excused?"

"You may. Go get your baths. *I* will clean up."

They agreed.

Later, Jake made Livy watch for him by the open door while he ran into his room to get his pillow. Other than that, he'd decided he wouldn't set foot in there. They wished they could explain about evil ghosts to Granny, but she was so worked up over her precious Celebration, they knew she'd never listen.

"You can sleep on my rug," Livy had said. "There's an extra blanket in my closet."

"Umm," he'd said, trying to decide. Would it be cowardly of him to sleep on the lavender rug of a girl's bedroom?

He figured he could live with it.

They turned out the light early so Granny wouldn't come checking on them and fuss some more. It was so strange, Jake thought, to live in a family where some members were constantly leaning backwards, toward the Old South, and others were leaning forward. He and Livy were like Mom, it seemed, feeling closed in by the great house and its traditions, and trusting the Yankees on television more than their own granny.

Jake heard Livy breathing deeply. Neither of them had mentioned the ghosts, and he had known by her eyes that she didn't want him to. Still, he was surprised she had gotten to sleep so soon. He closed his eyes.

Maybe this is all a dream, he thought, listening to the quiet.

There was a single footstep directly above his head.

CHAPTER FOUR

Forbidden Ground

Jake got up quickly, and stood listening in the dark
room. There was just enough light to scan the stuffed
bears and seals and unicorns and dolls, all wide-eyed and
silent.

There was no other sound from above. They're playing with me, he thought. Or they're after me. It made
him angry that they wouldn't let him sleep—after all,
he'd given them his own room!

Jake left Livy sleeping and went to his door, opened
it wide and walked to his dresser. He pulled out jeans,
shirt and socks, keeping his mind on his task, trying not
to listen to the ceiling.

At last he was dressed; he pulled on a jacket, and eased
out the door. There was a light downstairs—Granny
must be up reading, he thought. He was painfully slow
on the stairs, avoiding all the creaky steps he knew so
well.

Sure enough, he saw her in the living room, working her way through a huge stack of women's magazines.

Jake had his own key to the sun-room door, and he managed to get outside without disturbing his grandmother. He tried not to think about what he was going to do.

In the storeroom there was a big spotlight. He got it out, tested it, then stepped into the garden.

The moon was two nights before the full, and ragged bright clouds drifted rapidly across it, thin and high above the black magnolias. Snatches of the boxwood paths were lit.

As Jake walked to the boarded-up cave door, he tried to figure out just what was making him so mad. It wasn't only the intrusion of ghosts into his house; their bumping and crunching on his ceiling was almost comic, as if they'd seen a lot of television and decided to try out the tricks. But what harm could such ghosts do?

He walked slowly up to the boarded door. A single shaft of moonlight penetrated the thick trees, and lay across the weathered wood like a bar of tarnished silver.

Well, Jake said to himself, here I am. And suddenly he knew what was making him angry. He had a secret fear that he didn't even like to tell himself about, much less anyone else. He wondered whether he was brave enough—as brave as he should be. Some boys his age didn't seem to mind getting in fights, but he avoided all situations that were about to lead that way. But should he? And why did he have to think think think so much, about everything, before he was ready to act? It was as if the ghosts were trying to scare him, just as a test, taunting and teasing like bullies on the playground at school.

How he hated that playground: the ground worn to fine dust by generations of little feet, the slim elm trees rubbed smooth as the rungs of monkey bars by the hands that swung on them, around and endlessly around; the pecking order of kids at recess—big and mean, down to the smallest and most vulnerable, with himself somewhere in the middle. Oh, he was popular enough, but he felt so uneasy with the school mob, not quite fitting into the games, for some reason he'd never understood. And so, watching hard tackle football, he would wonder whether he was basically chicken because he didn't want to play. And did the other kids know that? Is that why they didn't invite him?

He kicked the boarded door of the cave.

"Anybody home?" he said.

But he didn't say it as loudly as he wished he had, and so found himself as unhappy as before, and angrier, because the spirits seemed to call for more and more tests, and he couldn't imagine himself finally being brave enough, and proving it once and for all.

"Help!"

It was a weak cry within the cave.

Now Jake was really afraid.

"Where are you?" It was a little girl's voice, sounding frightened.

"Over here!" Jake cried.

Then he was scared by how loud he'd been, and he

looked all around, expecting anything, from Granny to a spirit.

He listened to the silence. It was still too cool at night for crickets and cicadas. The slight breeze brought a little rattle from broad stiff magnolia leaves.

"Can you hear me?" Jake said to the door, more quietly now.

When there was no response he kicked it again, and waited. But still there was nothing.

He waited as long as he could stand it.

Finally he headed for the house, his thoughts turning over and over, trying to decide what to do. This must be Darcy!

Granny was gone to her room; Jake slipped up to Livy with scarcely a crack from the floorboards.

Then he shook her gently. But she wouldn't wake up; she was sleeping hard. Finally, she was fighting him off and then sitting up saying, "What? What?"

"Livy! She's in the tunnel! Right under our house!"

"Who?"

"Darcy! I heard her. Are you awake?"

"Just a minute," she said, opening and closing her eyes. Jake explained the whole thing.

"Well," Livy said, "it must be her."

"I know. But she seems to be lost in there."

"Sarantha should be able to find her, don't you think?"

"Yes. I don't know why she hasn't already."

"I don't think it's *our* business, Jake."

"I know. But you should have *heard* her. She sounded so pitiful."

"Hmmm."

"Maybe we ought to open that door," Jake said. "Just to let her out."

"Ghosts don't need doors, do they?"

"Who knows, Livy? Maybe they do, for some reason."

"Is Mom home?"

"No, silly! You haven't been asleep long. Look, come with me, and I'll open the tunnel door."

There was silence in the room while Livy thought it over.

"Okay," she said.

She didn't sound scared or concerned to Jake, just a little excited and amused. This irritated him, but at the same time he couldn't blame her—even now it was hard to believe there were really ghosts. At any moment, he felt, all these happenings would simply stop, forever.

Soon they were both outside, and Jake rummaged in the toolshed for the long crowbar.

"You better not wake Granny," Livy said as he felt along the door seam with the flat end of the bar.

"Shhhh," he whispered. "The wood is soft."

He hooked the crooked end under a wide board nailed across the door, and came down on it with all his weight.

The old nails squeaked and slid free.

He pulled the board off with his hands.

Then he fitted the flat end between the door and its frame, and shoved hard against the crook.

The gray wood splintered. He felt for another spot,

and tried again. This time there was a loud crack and the door opened about an inch. A strange smell poured out like breath.

"I can do it," he said, jamming the crowbar into the space.

Soon he had the door standing half open. He put the bar down and shined his spotlight inside.

The cave was smaller than he'd always thought it would be, and reminded him of the small Civil War uniforms he had seen—and for that matter the small suits of medieval armor in museums—and he wondered for an instant if the slaves who dug this tunnel were smaller than present-day people. In any case, the space was unpleasant-looking, and it quickly curved away, down deeper into the earth.

"Okay," Livy said, "we've done our part."

"Yeah."

"So, let's go back inside." Livy rubbed her eye. "Jake," she said, yawning, "I can't believe you waked me up for this."

"Couldn't see you missing the fun," he said.

"Well, any more ideas you get tonight, you just go ahead without me."

"All right," he said, taking a step closer to the cave opening, and shining the beam around.

"I wonder where Darcy is," he said. "You know it would be an awful shame to miss seeing her, if we could."

"I guess."

"Let's wait here a few minutes, okay?"

"Well, not long; I'm chilly."

"It's just . . ."

He took a step inside. To his surprise, he wasn't frightened.

"Jake, no! Now don't do that."

"It's so weird," he said, searching the rough clay walls and the hand-cut beams. "She was deeper—much deeper inside."

"Come back, Jake!"

But he was already walking slowly along, moving the light. He liked Livy's fearing for him.

"What are you *doing?*" Livy asked, her voice on the rise.

"Just wait a minute," Jake said quietly. "I'm only having a look . . ."

With that he disappeared around the first curve. He saw that the cave narrowed even more. Was a little girl really down in there? He was afraid to leave, because it was easier to believe a *real* child was somehow inside than to think it was a ghost. Imagine trying to explain why he ignored the pleas of a flesh-and-blood girl! That would be much worse than telling the family he took the cries of a ghost seriously.

"Jake!" Livy said. "This isn't funny!"

She must not even believe me, he thought, or she'd be worried about the little girl, too.

Soon he came to the site of an old cave-in, and saw a rough beam lying where it had fallen from the roof, with a mound of rubble over it nearly blocking the tunnel. A bare end sticking out showed why it had fallen: it was wormed with termite holes.

Jake stepped over the mess, through the small hole,

and noticed that the sharp, mildewy smell of the cave became stronger.

His foot went down on the dark side of the mound, landing on a dry stick which cracked like a shot.

Livy screamed and came running after him, and he raised his voice to tell her he was not hurt. But she never heard him because at that moment the big door crashed, slamming, behind her. He pulled his foot back, trying to figure why she'd done that, but he knew from her screaming that she hadn't. He ran toward her and they hit each other in the passage, and he kept saying it's all right, it's all right, over and over and over. When they were finally calm enough, they went back to try the door.

It was sealed tightly, as far as they could tell; in fact it seemed to be nailed shut, for all they could budge it in try after try.

"I can't stand it in here!" Livy cried. "I can't stand the air!"

"Calm down, now," he said. "It'll be all right, I promise."

He put his arm around her.

"Oh, great," she said, shivering against him, "you promise."

"All we have to do," he said, "is listen for Mom in the driveway. When she gets out, and starts for the house, we'll yell for her, and she'll hear us."

"Do you think she will?"

"Sure. I heard Darcy, didn't I? And she was way *way* down in the cave."

"I guess so."

"Don't worry, Liv," he said, patting her on the shoulder.

So they sat and waited in the darkness for three hours, saving their spotlight batteries, and getting tired.

They were leaning against each other, almost asleep, when they finally heard their mother's car.

The car door clicked shut, and they were on their feet.

Then they clearly heard their mother's footsteps coming down the path. When she reached the stairs and started up they knew she was at the point nearest them.

"Mom!" they cried together.

"Mom! Mom! We're in *here!* Down below, in the cave! Can you hear us? Mom! We can hear *you!*"

But the house door slammed.

Faintly, they made out the bolt turning in the lock.

"What's wrong with her?" Livy asked angrily. "How come we can hear her so well, and she can't hear us?"

"I don't know," Jake said thoughtfully.

"Has she got her mind on her history papers? Is that her problem?"

Livy sounded mad enough to smash down the door.

"I don't think so," Jake said quietly. "I don't think that's it."

CHAPTER FIVE

A Charming Spirit

They listened in the musty darkness. Jake hugged Livy and felt her heart racing where his hand touched the vein in her neck. He wondered whether she felt his heart.

"Why didn't she hear us?" Livy said again. "Why didn't she?"

"Shhhh. I'm thinking."

"Do you think a ghost locked us in here?"

"Uh . . ." Jake didn't want to answer.

"And kept her from hearing?"

"Livy . . ."

"Yes?"

"Let's see if the light works."

It did.

"If it *is* what we think," he said, "they must want us to go deeper in the cave. That's all I can figure out."

"To the timegate? But Sarantha said nobody can go through it."

"Well, *she* wouldn't do this to us." Jake said. "It

44

must be those creeps in the attic, for some reason we don't know."

"Maybe they want to kill us."

"Shhhh. No. They could have done that by now—if they were able to slam that door."

"Oh, yeah."

"We might as well play along," Jake said, pointing his beam down in the tunnel.

"No! I don't think so, Jake. Not in a million years!"

"Look. This could be nothing—just a series of accidents, right?" He cut off the light to save it while he argued.

"Maybe."

"Okay. In that case, we might find another way into the house, or up to the garden. It won't hurt to look. And if somebody—or some thing—did this to us, we'll just find out what they wanted. Maybe we can help Darcy."

"Jake, sometimes it seems like you *want* something to happen."

"Honestly, Liv, if we could help her, and get back out of this cave, I would like that."

She didn't reply, and he couldn't see her face. Had he frightened her? Was she going to cry?

But she touched his arm lightly.

"Okay, brother. I guess you're right. Lead the way."

Jake was surprised—and he was glad she couldn't see his expression. She was looking up to him!

So he followed his spotlight down into the earth, moving slowly, feeling Livy clutching the back of his jacket.

When they came to the cave-in he worked through the hole first, then he held the light down on the floor for her to follow, over the mound of dirt.

They started again, and the hole slanted deeper down. Jake noticed that the ground was covered with a layer of fine dust, and there were no human footprints in it. Whoever that voice belonged to either hadn't come this far, or didn't leave tracks. He shivered.

It occurred to Jake that they might come to the timegate somewhere in the cave, and he wondered how it worked—if you touched it with one finger, would your whole body go through?

And he got his answer. There was a rush of wind and he felt himself shooting weightlessly down a dark space, holding desperately to Livy's hand behind him in the emptiness. His spotlight was gone.

Then he was standing on solid earth, weaving a bit, catching his balance, still feeling Livy's warm and tight grip.

They were in a vast field, a grassy cool pasture, and overhead arched a dome of bright clear night stars.

There was a different silence here, and he stepped closer to his sister and whispered, sensing that he shouldn't make a sound.

"Are you all right?"

"Yes," she said softly.

"The timegate."

"Oh, Jake . . . It's *true!*"

"Yeah."

"This is the below-world. It must have been Darcy you heard!"

"But it's crazy," he said. "I heard her, but Mom couldn't hear us. It doesn't make any sense."

"Don't worry about that right now," Livy said.

"Why not?" he asked, annoyed. He was just thinking they'd better talk about everything that happened so they wouldn't miss any idea.

"Because look!" she whisper-yelled, pointing across the pasture.

There was a small silver spot moving toward them in the distance.

Jake felt his throat tighten and his stomach flutter.

"What's that? he said.

"I don't know!" she said, irritated. "But I'll tell you what we'd better do."

"What?"

"Mark this spot, and then hide."

"Uh, yeah."

He turned around and around, but couldn't find a landmark to remember the timegate by. So he dug his heel into the soft dirt, making an X, and they held hands and ran.

They crossed most of the grassy field fast, heading for a jagged outline of dark woods, and they kept looking at the moving silver spot. It jingled as it angled toward them, and now they heard hoofbeats, too.

It was a rider, starlight reflecting off some of his gear. Did he see them?

They ran harder, and now the grass was above their knees, wet with dew, thick and matted. A breeze swept over them and the grasstops sang. The air was sweet.

The hoofbeats were muted as they came on. Jake and

Livy had to slow down; their legs were tired, they were short of breath, and now the rider surely spotted them, for he changed course and bore down.

Jake stopped, holding Livy back, and he stood straight up, gathering his dignity, preparing to bluff whoever was approaching.

The figure arrived, a tall man on a fine horse, wearing the gray uniform of the old Confederacy and an officer's hat and sword.

He was fierce and elegant, with a long military moustache as blond as his flowing hair. He seemed to gather bits of silver starlight into himself, and to radiate a faint glow.

"My heaven," he said in a rich, courtly voice. "What children are these?"

Jake wasn't sure if he was speaking to them, but there wasn't anyone else about.

"I'm Jake James, sir. And this is my sister, Olivia."

Jake never used her formal name, but somehow he was sure this was the time.

"White children, in my pasture!" he declared. "This beats all!"

"How are you, Colonel Ruffin, sir?"

He raised his thick blond eyebrows and smiled.

"You know me, boy?"

"Of course, sir."

Jake was floating, reaching for anything he could say.

"And how can this be? I've been here a long long time, and I've never seen *you*."

"Of course not, sir. Why, ever since the War, Olivia

and I have lived over there in the woods, in our cave. We try not to bother anybody."

"I say!" the colonel snorted. He was so surprised he couldn't be still, and he turned his horse in a complete circle.

"This bears examination!" he finally said. "Why are you two out here in my pasture, in the middle of the night?"

Jake felt he was about out of answers.

"We get tired of staying in the woods all the time," Livy said, coming to the rescue. "We just *love* to look at the stars."

"Yes," the colonel said in his warm voice, sweeping his long arms to the heavens, "God's country, no question of it."

Soon Jake and Livy found themselves riding with him, mashed together uncomfortably behind his saddle, headed for his "big house," as he called it.

They passed silently along a dark woods trail, and began a gradual climb. When they emerged from the trees they saw a plantation house rising on a low hill, and Livy pinched Jake hard on both sides of his middle. He heard her gasp in his ear. And he wanted to say something, too, because it was their own house! It had the same roof line, the same high chimney—it had to be theirs. Only their garden trees and shrubs seemed different.

The colonel rode around back, stopped at a tall wooden post with a bell and rang it.

"Hop down, children," he said.

They slid over the hot smooth horse's rump to the ground.

A tall thin man, dignified and graceful and old, came walking from the house.

"Take the reins, William. Walk my mare about the grounds, put the tack away, feed her for the night and hurry back inside. I want tea for these children, possibly something more."

"Yas, suh," the man said.

The colonel led them up the back stairs, and they glanced at each other silently, amazed, feeling the solid steps and railing of their own house set back a century and more in time.

The colonel took off his riding boots and hat and sword, and tossed them onto a plump crimson chair.

Jake and Livy looked around—none of the furniture was the same, or the pictures on the walls, but the rooms were identical in size and shape. The room was richly furnished, with thick embroidered curtains, overstuffed chairs and daybeds and shining walnut and mahogany tables. It was lit with softly burning lamps, their silver bases bright beneath slender glass chimneys.

"This house," the colonel said gravely, "is an island of sanity in a world gone mad."

"It is?" Jake said.

"My, yes," he said, closing his eyes for emphasis. "It's one of the few places the Yankees haven't wrecked, in one way or the other."

The children looked at each other—if he didn't sound like Granny!

"I'll bet you two are hungry," Colonel Ruffin said in a kind voice.

"I am," Jake quickly put in.

"I suppose I could eat a little something," Livy said.

"Fine, Miss Olivia! As soon as William comes in I'll have him fix up two plates. He's a good cook, you know."

"He's your cook and he takes care of your horse, too?" Livy asked.

"Indeed yes," the colonel said, smiling. "William is a mighty talented slave. But don't you ever tell him I said so!"

CHAPTER SIX

When Ghosts Tell Lies

Jake and Livy almost smiled at each other—his slave? How ridiculous could somebody be? And yet, of course it made sense, if they were really back in time.

The colonel beamed, as if they just delighted him.

"You're wondering," he said, "how it can be that I still have a slave, after the War is over with—aren't you?"

"Uh, yes," Jake said.

"The answer is that *I* never surrendered! In fact, *never* is my favorite word!"

He laughed loudly and held his stomach.

"But . . ." he said, quickly under control, "I have to be careful. My plantation is isolated to some degree . . . but the Yankees are always prowling about."

"They are?"

"It's their nature, son. They're always butting in. They're not like us here in the South, as you well know. We had a way of life like nothing in the world. It freed the better class of us for the finer things, while it kept the slaves busy and out of trouble—oh, perfect system! The blacks themselves were happy. Anyone who ever heard them singing down in the quarters would realize that, except Yankees. They're too coldhearted."

"Granny says the same thing," Livy said. She looked at Jake, then quickly back at the colonel. "I mean, she used to."

"A fine woman, I have no doubt. Tell me how you came to be separated from your kinfolks. And why on *earth* haven't you introduced yourselves before now?"

Jake hoped Livy would carry this story, since she had started it.

"When the War ended," she said in a thick, sugary voice, "we were left orphans, uh, up near Shiloh."

"No!" the colonel said.

Jake looked at him closely. He seemed so sincere and warm, so concerned about them.

"Yes, sir," Livy continued. "The Yankees had done away with Mama and Papa and Granny, and we had to run just to save our lives."

"The Federals were everywhere," Jake put in.

"I know what you mean," Colonel Ruffin said, "I surely do."

"Yes," Jake added with enthusiasm, "and the carpet-baggers, too. They had the morals of rattlesnakes!"

Livy gave him a quick glance—this was a favorite saying of Granny's.

"Finally we came to your woods," Livy said, "and found a little cave. We were just afraid to show our faces."

"Land to goodness," the colonel said, "to think of such

suffering, right here in my own brier patch, so to say. Well, you little darlings have found refuge at last, that's what. Welcome to Tapalyla Hill."

"Oh, we know it well," Jake blurted out, "it's a great place."

"You do? How?"

"Uh, well . . ."

"And *why* didn't you come to me before? Couldn't you see I was your own kind?"

"We . . ." Livy began uncertainly.

"I tried to tell them what a generous man you was."

William was speaking from the doorway. He had a high and careful voice.

"I showed them the house, an' I told them you was quality, Colonel, suh, but they said they mama an' they papa done warned them about any an' all."

The colonel's face flushed red.

"Why is it," he said loudly, "that they came to *you*, and not to *me*?"

"Suh," William continued, seeming not to notice the colonel's tone or Livy and Jake's puzzled faces. "I came upon them once in the woods, surprised them, like, an' I gave them a little chicken to eat. After that, they put theys trust in me."

"Oh," the colonel said, running this through his mind a few times while the others waited in silence.

Jake and Livy looked questioningly at William, grateful that he had filled out their story.

William closed his eyes and rocked back gently on his heels.

The colonel at last nodded, distracted and troubled, as if he were sympathetic and angry about their plight. Jake wondered when he could talk with William alone.

"What about food?" Colonel Ruffin said.

"I got it ready, suh," William replied.

"Very good."

Colonel Ruffin led them into the big kitchen as he stuffed his brier pipe. He sat down beside them, lit up and crossed his long legs.

The meal was hardly "a little something," as Livy had requested. They had cold partridge with wild rice, hot biscuits with butter and honey and sassafras tea.

The colonel sat with glowing eyes, as if fascinated by them, and pleased with his own hospitality.

"Jake," he said, "I've got the finest pointing dogs in this county. And more coveys of quail than you could shoot in three winters! I'm telling you boy, you're going to like it around here."

"Sounds great, sir." Jake wondered why the colonel, like his father, assumed he was dying to hunt.

"And I've got an English shotgun, a twin-hammer double, eleven gauge. Now—I can't wait to see if you're man enough to handle it."

"Yes, sir."

"Ah, yes, this is the life. Right, William?"

"Sho' is," William answered thinly from the stove.

"You see, children," Colonel Ruffin said, exhaling his rich pipe tobacco, "the plantation life is what makes everybody the most comfortable. We have our proper roles—what we're suited for—and we have the finest manners on the globe. The point of that, of course, is that everybody always knows how to act! A great blessing, as you will see if you ever visit a northern city."

"That's what Granny always said," Livy added.

"Oh, yes; a perceptive lady, no doubt."

Jake's eyelids were heavy, and the colonel noticed it.

"We'll talk in the morning," he said cheerfully. "Come along now and I'll show you your rooms."

The colonel led them to adjoining bedrooms—their own rooms!—and bade them good night.

Jake waited fifteen minutes, as long as he could stand it, and slipped to Livy's door.

He tapped twice and went inside.

"Shhh!" she said.

He made a face at her.

"Listen," he said, "we've got to figure this out. Do you believe we're really back in time?"

"How do I know? We've got to talk to that William."

"Yeah."

"I wonder where he sleeps."

"Probably out back, in the slave quarters."

"Did you see them?"

"No, but in *our* yard there's the old brick foundation of them, remember?"

"Oh—behind the garden."

"That's right. We'll wait a while and then go there."

"Okay. Colonel Ruffin didn't seem that bad, did he?" Livy asked.

"No . . . But he's a little scary underneath, somehow. And if half of what Sarantha said is true . . ."

"Sarantha said nobody from above could pass through the timegate, too, didn't she?"

"Right. That's what I heard. So maybe she was lying about other things," Jake admitted.

"Colonel Ruffin felt so sorry for us," Livy said.

"Yeah. You'd think he could tell we aren't ghosts, wouldn't you?"

Livy thought it over.

"Yes," she said slowly, "he seems to believe we're like him, whatever that is."

They eased down the steps and out the back door. By following familiar paths in the garden, they soon reached a small brick house in the trees. A yellow glow lit the window, and Jake knocked lightly.

"I'm here!" William said.

His steps were quick and he swung open the door, grinning. He was missing about half his teeth.

"I knowed y'all was comin'!" he said, quickly closing the door behind them. "Y'all such a sight fo' these old eyes!"

"We are?" Jake said. "Why?"

"Cause you the las' chance, thas why. This so-called world comin' to the end of itself day after tomorrow. If you don't show me the way to that timegate, I'm gone with the rest of 'em."

"You know where we come from?" Livy said. "And what we are?"

"Sho' do," he said with a twinkle, "I knowed Sarantha would send somebody."

"So it's all true!" Jake cried. "Does Colonel Ruffin have slaves locked in the basement?"

William turned away from them. He licked his paper-thin lips in a nervous way, and seemed tied in a knot.

"William?" Livy asked.

"Yas, ma'am?"

"Are they still down there? In the cages?"

"I reckon so," he said in his high voice, not meeting her eyes.

"You and Darcy never found the courage for another try," Jake said.

"Sho' ain't," he whispered.

"And you want us to help you out of here . . . leaving them behind?"

William rubbed his long hands together.

"Look here," he finally said. "Y'all don't know how it is, tryin' to keep 'live 'roun that man. I ain't seen Darcy in years an' years; she stay in the terrible swamp, an' I can't blame her none. The bes' we can do is go straight to that gate this minute, an' save ourselves."

"But if you fail to save your friends," Livy said, "what will you gain? Won't you have to do all this again? Have another contract with the colonel and all?"

"I 'speck so," he said. "I be willin' to do mos' anythin' later on; if I can just get far far 'way from him fo' a while, an' get me some res'."

Livy shook her head.

"Don't judge," William said, "'less you knows what the other man's burden truly be."

"I don't understand something," Jake said. "Sarantha sent us to help you out? Is that what you said before?"

"Un-huh."

"So she was lying—saying nobody could pass through the timegate?"

William's sad eyes smiled.

"The truth is, she can't pass it no mo'. She part of the contract to stay 'way, an' let Darcy make it on her own."

"But we're not?" Jake asked.

"No, suh. Y'all ain't supposed to be here, an' really, Sarantha done tricked you into comin'. But you might as well save me, since you can."

Livy laughed quickly.

"We might as well save Darcy, too," she said.

"Y'all never find that child," he said. "She keep in the river swamp. I wouldn't go there fo' nothin'."

He pointed toward the gardens and beyond. Jake knew where he meant; it was the same great woods where, in his own world, his father loved to hunt turkeys.

"If you're so scared," Livy said, "how can you act this calm?"

Now William's eyes were heavy lidded, almost sleepy.

"Thas mah trick, child. Thas how I handles the colonel all day long—how I keeps off them rages of his."

"Rages?" Jake asked.

"He been known to break chairs over top the table, chop down his fruit trees an' shoot his own bird dog when it bit down a little hard on a quail."

"And kill people," Livy said.

William gazed at her, and finally just nodded.

"Well," Jake said, moving to the door, "we'll come back for you, William, if we can."

"Y'all ain't gon' to the swamp?"

"We've come this far," Livy said, "we might as well try."

They glanced at each other.

"You say we have two days?" Jake asked.

"At the mos'. Look right here."

He picked up a flatiron and mashed it between his hands, flattening it like soft lead. Then he broke it in half.

"Yesterday," he said, "this thing was solid an' hard. I'm tellin' you, we near the end."

"We'll hurry," Jake said.

William shook his head in disappointment as they left.

In the privacy of the dark garden trees they stopped to whisper.

"This whole place," Jake said, "is some kind of an illusion."

"Yeah. Maybe we should run straight for the time-gate. Sarantha tricked us—we don't owe her anything."

"But if we could find Darcy . . ."

"I know, I know . . . at least let's hurry if we're going to look. I don't want to get trapped in here."

"Me either." Jake shivered.

They were glad they had each other as they started for the terrible swamp.

CHAPTER SEVEN

To the River Swamp

They slipped between the cool hedges and ran into the woods. Jake had a fair idea of where Darcy's swamp was. They would have to find the river and cross it.

There were glimpses of moonlight where the trees allowed, and the paths seemed about the same as Jake remembered. He and Livy hurried, and it wasn't long before they stood on the Tapalyla's bank.

"Now what do we do?" Livy said. "There's no bridge in this time."

"Shhh," he said. "We'll walk along the shore until we find a boat. Then we'll borrow it."

But the land was wild—there were briers and tangles of honeysuckle vines—and no rowboats appeared. They trudged slowly along for an hour, moving upstream, and finally Jake spotted a strange object. They came closer, and saw that it was a raft, tied to a tree, and a long pole lay beside it in the grass.

"This will do!" Jake said.

He seized the rope and untied it, and in another moment they were moving down the surface of the silent river.

"How will you know when to go ashore?" Livey asked.

"I'm not sure."

"Oh, great. What if we drift right past the colonel's plantation?"

"I'm doing the best I can," Jake said. "Do you have a better idea?"

"I guess not," she said in a small voice.

"You sound teary," Jake said. "If you want to go through with this, you can't be crying."

"You made your point; now just hush and paddle this thing!"

"I'm not paddling, I'm poling."

"Whatever."

"Don't say that!" Jake snapped. "Daddy always says he hates that word because it's so imprecise."

Livy refused to answer. She looked out at the silvery passing bank, a moving line of moonlight on mud, and wished she had never come to this awful world.

She reached down and felt the edge of the raft, and closed her fingers. Sure enough, a piece of the oak crumbled without much pressure. It was true—this place was going to pieces fast. She started to tell Jake but kept silent.

After a long time they drifted around a bend and past a sand bar, and there stood a huge mournful cow, watching them come.

"We might be opposite the plantation," Livy said.

"Yeah."

"I think it's been long enough, don't you?"

"I guess."

"Well—shouldn't we go hunt for Darcy?"

"Let's drift downstream a little farther, Liv. In our world this swamp really gets started a mile or so south of town."

"This is hopeless," Livy said. "We don't even know where to start."

Then the trees began to overhang the river in an ominous way. Dark matted limbs reached out like arms, and bare roots spread from the bank in an overlapping maze. There was the strong smell of sulfurous marsh and decaying leaves.

"It feels different here," Livy said.

"Yeah. I think this is the big swamp."

He poled over to the bank, stood up and hopped ashore. He pulled the rope again, bringing Livy near, and told her to come on. But she was a little afraid of the step, and the raft drifted back into the current a bit.

"Oh, come on and jump," Jake said impatiently.

He pulled her nearer again.

She made one long step and hovered for a moment— a foot on land and a foot on the raft—and when she felt the gap widening she kicked off hard and jumped right into Jake. He tumbled down under her.

"Good grief, Livy," he said as he pushed her off and climbed to his feet. "I let go of the rope!"

They both stood still and watched the raft float away, out in the river where Livy had kicked it.

"You're so stupid!" he said angrily.

Livy had both fists at her mouth.

She almost jumped in the water after the raft.

"That's great, Livy," Jake said. "Now we'd *better* be in the right place."

She followed him as he felt his way along the high, brushy bank, searching for a path to the top. She was usually so careful; things like this just didn't happen to her.

Then he was climbing, and she followed holding onto roots and vines, not minding the scratches of briers in her anger, pulling herself up easily.

Soon they were in open woods full of moonlight, and they were walking away from the river.

They came to a great slough of still, black water, and heard snakes sliding in the buttonbushes and turtles plopping in from their rotten logs.

"It's so real," Livy said.

"What do you mean?"

"It's like the swamp Daddy took us to once, on a picnic, remember?"

"Yeah."

"You wouldn't ever think this world was about to end, would you?"

"No. I keep forgetting, too."

"Do you think we should yell for Darcy now?" Livy asked.

"*Yell* for her?"

"I don't see what else we could try."

They stood in the darkness, thinking. Jake slapped at a mosquito humming in his ear. In the distance an owl hooted its hollow call.

"Wait—I've got a better idea," Livy said. "Yelling might scare her off, so why don't we sing? If she hears us maybe she'll come close; we'll sing something she'll like."

"But what?"

In a moment Livy had it: *"Darcy, Darcy, Darcy girl, Sarantha says to leave this world; if you'll come and be our friend, we'll take you to her again."*

"That's great," Jake said.

"I'm glad you like it."

They set off walking very slowly in the swamp's darkness, stepping in cold wet holes and catching spider webs on their faces, holding hands and singing the little song. They were soon good and lost.

"I'm hungry," Jake said after a while.

"Me, too," Livy replied, "but so what?"

"Yeah. We should have brought something from that kitchen."

So on and on they went, singing until they grew hoarse.

A pale gray light spread through the trees around them, coming from nowhere but very slowly increasing.

"What's this?" Jake whispered, suddenly frightened.

"I think it's dawn," Livy said wearily.

"Oh, yeah."

"We can get our directions now," she said, "when the sun comes up."

Once the eastern sky broke with cracks and then bands of lavender and orange light, they turned and headed north.

"What I wouldn't give for some breakfast," Jake said.

"Keep singing," Livy said. "Remember what's going to happen to this world."

"You're right."

So they pushed on, seeking the swampiest places to try, and singing the little song. They invented different harmonies to fight the boredom.

The birds sang in the morning chorus as sunlight penetrated gloomy trees, and they were so loud Jake began to shout.

"Darcy, Darcy, Darcy girl!" he yelled in his scratchy voice. But he was interrupted.

"Hush, hush, don't sing so loud; land, you two sound mighty proud."

Jake and Livy were completely still. So were the birds.

"Who said that?" Livy whispered.

They heard giggling and a rustle of brush.

In a few moments, from a little distance, they heard: *"How you know my mama's name? Tell me why y'all really came!"*

"Darcy!" Jake and Livy said together.

They rushed in her direction.

But she kept ahead of them, singing her own ditties, and leading them deeper and deeper into the swamp.

"If only we could see her," Jake said.

"You don't understand," Livy cried hoarsely, "we've *got* to talk with you!"

"Y'all sho' sound like blood and flesh; tired while a little old ghost is fresh!"

Darcy gave a quick high giggle.

Jake and Livy stopped and looked at each other. They

were out of breath, hot and drippy, scratched and sore, hungry and tired.

"We're trying to help you!" Jake yelled angrily. "If you don't want to last, then we'll just go back!"

"Jake," Livy said, "you might frighten her."

"I mean it," he said. "This is too hard. She's probably flying along over the ground," he said, kicking a gnarly tree root and breaking it off. "If she doesn't want to be saved, there's nothing we can do."

"Yeah. We'll be lucky if we can make it to the time-gate ourselves," Livy said as she reached down for the piece of root Jake had kicked. She took it between her finger and thumb, and pinched it in half.

"Look, Jake—things are getting crumblier all the time."

"Darcy!" he yelled. "This is your last chance! Either come and talk with us now, or we're leaving, and you'll never see your mother again!"

They waited a few moments, listening.

A black wasp sailed past Jake's face.

In the distance, a gang of crows fussed over something.

The smell of swamp mud was overpowering.

"Let's go," Jake said at last.

"Okay."

Instantly, a small black girl—about eight years old—materialized before them.

"Darcy!" they cried.

"Sho' am. Now who all is y'all?"

"First," Jake said with controlled anger, "why didn't you come to us before?"

"I was testin' y'all," she said. "You could have been Colonel Ruff, thas who. A devil like him can take whatever form he likes—you know that."

"He can?" Livy said.

"Where you see my mama?" Darcy asked.

"In the above-world," Jake sighed. "And this world's coming to its end. Or do you know that? Everybody else here seems to."

Up to this point Darcy had seemed clever and tireless, almost comfortable, like a wild animal in the swamp. But suddenly she was out of words. Tears leaked down her round cheeks, and her shoulders sagged. She gazed into the trees.

"We gon' perish. I knows that."

"But, Darcy," Livy said softly, "all we have to do is go through the timegate. We can take you there."

"I know where it is," Darcy said tearfully. "I'se suppose' to help some folks out. But it was too hard! It wasn't fair!"

Livy held out her arms and Darcy went to her.

"It wasn't fair! It wasn't fair!" Darcy said between sobs.

"Nobody said life was fair," Jake said, quoting Granny.

CHAPTER EIGHT

A Frightened Ghost

Once Darcy cried she seemed to feel better. She kept holding Livy's hand and smiling at her. Jake watched silently, trying to imagine a hundred years alone, and how good the touch of another person would feel after that.

Suddenly Darcy took off, leading them to a well-worn path, chopped by deer tracks and rabbit prints.

They came to a rickety bridge over a deep creek.

"Right here a place I hate," Darcy said.

"What do you mean?" Livy asked.

"If you think it's easy, you go in front."

Jake stepped ahead of them, staring down cautiously. He took the first step.

From down in the crevasse of the rocky creek there came a roar.

Jake jumped back off the bridge.

"What on earth is that?"

"Take a peek," Darcy said, grinning.

Jake looked over the edge, and finally spotted a long dark shape moving in the shallow water.

"Thas a bull 'gator," Darcy said. "See what I mean? You got to walk careful over this little bridge."

"I'll say you do," Livy said.

Darcy took her hand and pulled her out onto the bridge, and Jake followed quickly, wondering if an alligator ghost would eat you as quickly as a regular alligator would.

Soon they reached Darcy's cave.

It was at the foot of a hill, under the powerful exposed roots of a great beech tree. A campfire smoldered in the small clearing's center, with heavy limbs dragged around it for seats, and over at the side hung a swing of woven grapevines.

"You live here?" Livy asked, astonished.

"It's all right," Darcy said, "I likes it fine. Colonel Ruffin, he don't have no idea where we at."

"But do you know this place is going to be destroyed?" Jake asked.

"Sometime," she said, looking away.

"No," Livy said sternly, "not sometime. Tomorrow! And everybody here is going to be destroyed with it!"

Livy grabbed a loose stone and broke it over her knee. "See? Things are losing their strength already."

Jake stomped on the dirt and his foot crunched down several inches.

"Look at that," he said. "I could feel it earlier—the ground's getting like a great big pie crust."

"I knows the way out," Darcy said shyly.

"We know you do," Livy said. "Did you actually go through the timegate yesterday, and get lost in a dark tunnel?"

"Sho' did not!" Darcy said. "I ain't been away from this swamp since I don't know when!"

Jake and Livy faced each other.

"So," Jake said angrily, "it was Sarantha in the cave, disguising her voice."

"What a tricker!" Livy said.

"I sho' would love to see Mama again," Darcy said.

"I want to see her myself," Jake said. "I've got a few things to get straight with her."

"Y'all ain't scared to go past the colonel's?" Darcy asked.

"No," Jake answered, annoyed. "In fact, we're going back to the mansion and do what you were supposed to do a long time ago."

Darcy looked horrified.

Jake caught a glimpse of himself as Darcy must see him—brave and in charge. He liked that just fine. But it isn't really courage, he thought, as much as not being able to stand the way these ghosts act!

"Is y'all hungry?" Darcy asked in a dreamy voice.

Jake looked closely at her. She's drifted from fear to food, he thought, in two seconds. The poor girl's been out here alone so long, with her terrible memories and no future she could face up to . . . no wonder she hardly even acts sane.

"I'm starving," Jake said in a controlled voice, "but I have no intention of dying in this place, and I believe I can wait till I get home to eat."

"Why he yellin' at me?" Darcy asked as she hugged Livy. "I was just gon' fix y'all a sandwich."

"He's not yelling," Livy said, smoothing Darcy's hair back, "he's worrying about you. We have to go now— understand?"

Darcy sniffed and nodded. She wouldn't meet Jake's eyes, but she took Livy's hand and squeezed it.

"Lead us to the river as near the plantation as you can," Jake said.

"Fast," Livy whispered to her.

So off she went, running ahead but clutching Livy's hand. Within an hour they reached the river bank at a point opposite the colonel's land.

They lay hidden in the blackberry bushes, watching for signs of life.

"How do we get across?" Livy asked Darcy.

"I got a way," she said. "It ain't rained in a while, an' the river be low. The colonel, he lets them cows a his run loose 'round here. All we got to do is wait till it be dark, an' ride them cows across."

"Ride cows?" Jake said.

"Where do you find them?" Livy asked. Darcy pointed to a wooded flat upstream.

"Over in them trees," she said.

"We can't wait for night," Jake said. "We'll have to chance it now."

"I ain't doin' that," Darcy said.

"Yes, you are," Jake said.

"You know why we have to," Livy whispered, patting Darcy's hand.

Darcy stared at the far bank, squinted her eyes and

tightened her teeth and held her fists against her chest. She began to tremble in little shudders. Livy put her arms around her, and they both shook for a while. Slowly, the attack passed.

"I can do it," Darcy said. "If we goes right now."

They ran, and the acorn flat was indeed thick with fat black-and-white cows, munching wild grass in the deep shade. They seemed to know Darcy, and merely switched their tails and rolled their great eyes as she walked among them.

"This my favorite," she said, patting one. "Let's see can we all fit on."

They climbed aboard the broad back, with Darcy up front and Jake in back, and the slow lumbering cow began to ease them toward the sunlight.

She walked right into the gurgling water, and they held their feet up high. In the very middle of the river the cow stopped, and seemed to study the bright sun on the moving current, but Darcy pulled her ear and she continued on her way.

A few moments later they were standing on the other side. Darcy slid off and gave the cow a farewell pat.

"So far so good," Jake said, "now we've got to slip up to the house and let the other slaves go."

Darcy's face was trembling.

"Not you," he said. "We'll hide you at the edge of the woods—Livy can even stay with you—and I'll come back with the others."

Darcy wouldn't meet his eyes.

They crossed the plantation, staying out of sight in the hedgerows and wooded fence lines, but finally they were hunkered in hackberry shade, looking out on the broad green sunlit pasture.

Jake picked up a rock and crushed it to dust in his fingers.

"It won't be long," he whispered. "Wait here for me."

"I'm going," Livy said. "And as for you," she said to Darcy, "you'd better think carefully—this could be the chance you need . . . The very last one."

Darcy's dark dreamy eyes drifted across the field. Jake shook his head as he watched her.

"Look!" Livy said, pointing into the distance.

Far away there was a rising wisp of smoke or steam, spreading unevenly toward them.

"Whas that?" Darcy said.

"I don't know," Livy whispered.

"We studied volcanoes at school," Jake said. "Sometimes they start this way, with a crack in the earth."

"Oh, no," Livy said, "we really *are* near the end."

Another column of steam ran from the first one, as if a second crack had opened.

"We'd better leave *now*," Livy said. "All of us."

"I know," Jake said, "but I promised William."

They were silent for a moment, watching the rising steam, and Jake thought how strange it was that he had assumed Darcy's burden.

He decided to send his sister and Darcy through the timegate and run back alone, even if he had to fool them to do it. And he began to see why the slaves had to scheme.

"Come on," he said, running into the tall pasture grass.

They followed, but when Jake looked over his shoulder to check on them he saw the colonel charging from the woods on his horse.

He stopped and let the girls run past him. "Keep going!" he cried to Livy.

He faced Colonel Ruffin, who was grinning fiercely and swinging a long bullwhip over his head as he galloped.

"Cutting it mighty close, aren't you, boy?" he cried reigning up beside Jake.

Suddenly Jake turned and screamed, "Livy!"

She was running fast, straight for the timegate.

"Don't show him where it is!"

Jake was numb and falling, his chest stinging, and he was down in the grass hearing hoofbeats when he realized the colonel had hit him with the bullwhip.

He got to his knees, dazed, and watched Livy running at the wrong angle. Darcy had let go of her hand, and she was heading too far wide on the opposite side of the timegate. Livy must be doing it on purpose, he thought, and Darcy must not be sure where it is.

Now Jake was running, too, following the colonel and watching him waver between the two girls, jerking his horse this way and that, trying to decide which of them to stay with. On his present course Colonel Ruffin would fly right through the timegate!

But he chose Darcy, and bore down hard on her.

Livy looked back at Jake and he waved his arm toward the timegate, and she changed direction. Now they were converging; Jake's side was hurting but it wasn't far so he kept on running, scanning the ground ahead for any sign of the X he had made.

He glanced at Darcy. She was so small and desperately quick on her run; the big gray horse was almost on her.

Livy was nearly to Jake now, her arm outstretched, and he caught her fingers as he saw the *X* ahead.

Colonel Ruffin reached low as he came to Darcy, and his horse didn't even slow down as he swooped her up.

It was the last sight Jake and Livy saw as they vanished through the timegate.

CHAPTER NINE

But No One Believes

Jake and Livy were standing in the dark, breathing hard, holding hands, tottering for their balance.

Jake touched the cold dirt wall of the cave.

"We're back!" he said. "Don't let go of me, but bend down and feel for the spotlight."

"Okay."

In a moment she had it and switched it on.

"He got her," Livy breathed. "I saw him grab her up."

"I know. I *hate* him."

"Me, too! Oh, Jake—we came so close."

"I'd almost go back right now."

"*No!* You can't—you'd just show him the timegate."

"Yeah."

"Let's see if we can get out of here."

"Okay."

"We did our best," Livy said. "At least we know that."

"Maybe we did—I keep wondering if *I* did."

"Come on," she said.

They crossed the cave-in point, and followed the winding tunnel as it rose toward their house.

When the beam of light hit the door, it was standing a few inches open.

"Look!" Livy cried, rushing for it.

In a moment they were in their garden, giving thanks.

"Doesn't the air smell great?" Livy said, laughing and crying at the same time, and holding Jake's arms as she jumped up and down. "I *never* thought I'd see this world again!"

"Yeah," Jake said, grinning.

He wished he could celebrate as freely as his sister could. But he couldn't stop thinking about Darcy, and wondering what he had done wrong.

A group of dressed-to-kill ladies stood peering at Jake and Livy.

"Oh!" Livy said. "Who are you?"

"We," a confident spokeswoman said, "are the First Baptist Garden Club of Cedar Valley, darling. Who are you?"

"My goodness," Livy said wearily, "you're here for the tour."

"We are indeed! We've traveled a mighty long way on our charter bus for this event, and we expect to love every minute of it."

"You will," Livy said sarcastically.

"Just watch out for the ghosts," Jake added.

"Then it's true?" the woman said in a loud, thrilled voice.

She looked at her group and smiled with her tongue between her teeth.

The ladies hurried on toward the house, leaving Jake and Livy alone. They stood together feeling exhausted and depressed, not only having failed to save Darcy, but now being delivered to the world where people rushed about on silly errands, not knowing what things meant. There would be visitors like these until after the Celebration Ball.

Just then their mother came through the garden, and when they spotted her they ran and grabbed her arms.

"Mom!" Livy said. "We thought we'd never see you again!"

"You did? Why on earth?"

"Didn't you miss us?" Jake said, astonished.

"Where have you been?"

"Didn't you know we weren't in our beds all night? Didn't you notice we weren't there at breakfast?"

"Really? I'm sorry, dears, but I've had so much on my mind. I got home late and went right to sleep, and this morning I assumed you were avoiding all the excitement."

"You mean Granny," Livy said.

Their mother gave a worried smile.

"Well, we *weren't* home," Jake said. "Do you want to hear where we were?"

"Where?" She said it with a dutiful, amused air, rather than with the concern Jake expected.

"Through the timegate!" they cried together.

Their mother looked shocked; she turned back and

forth between them. But the way she was smiling, they knew she was only reacting to their performance.

"We're not kidding," Jake said calmly. "We went into the cave"—he pointed toward the tunnel door—"and it slammed behind us."

"Yes!" Livy said. "And we heard you come home last night, and park the car, and we screamed and screamed—see, the door was stuck—but you couldn't hear us."

"We only went in," Jake said, "because I heard a little girl's voice inside."

"Anyway," Livy continued, "once we were trapped in there, we went deeper and deeper, and then we suddenly popped into another world!"

"Honest, Mom! We did this!" Jake said.

They stopped.

By the look on her face, they could see the story was getting less believable all the time, with each detail.

"Really," Livy said, very quietly.

"Honestly," their mother laughed, "I thought for a minute there you *had* been somewhere all night."

"No, listen!" Livy said, trembling.

"*You* listen," their mother said sharply. "I'm going to be late for class if I don't leave right now—no, five minutes ago."

Quickly and very pleasantly, she kissed each of them on the cheek.

"Try that out on Granny," she said as she headed for her car, "she'll eat it up. Oh, I know—tell her you met her ghost in there!"

They put the spotlight in the shed and went in the

house. Granny was directing the garden club ladies through the sun room.

"No," she was saying, "the ghost hasn't shown herself in quite a long time, but there have been certain signs recently . . ."

"Oh, really? Do tell us!"

"Peculiar noises, knockings on the ceiling—particularly in my room—but when we go to investigate in the attic, no one's in sight."

Jake and Livy rolled their eyes at each other. They slipped into the kitchen behind Granny's back, and sat down glumly at the glass-topped table. Jake felt as though he would burst in the silence.

"Did you hear what she said?" he asked.

Livy nodded, looking like she might cry.

"I know she won't listen," Jake continued.

"No."

"I was so hungry, and now I don't even want to eat."

"Me either," Livy said. "I feel sick."

Granny appeared at the door.

"You!" she cried. "I called you for the nice hot breakfast I made, poached eggs and bacon and grits and biscuits, but, oh, no—you'd already dressed and left this house. Here I am trying to give the tours, upholding my duty as a member of this family, and you're sneaking around, getting ready to mess up the kitchen!"

"Are not," Jake said under his breath.

"We saw your ghost," Livy said bitterly, "and she's nothing like you imagine."

"Don't tell her," Jake said.

"I want to. I want her to know that her famous ghost

isn't Mrs. Ruffin at all . . . It's one of the black slaves who once belonged to the Ruffin family."

Granny's cheeks swelled. She worked a hard ball of air behind her tight lips, and flushed like a plum.

"You most certainly have not seen my ghost! What you have mainly not seen enough of is the paddle, the belt and the switch!"

"Yoo-hoo," the garden club ladies called.

"Coming, dears!" Granny sang in a perfectly happy voice, making her exit.

"She's crazy," Livy said.

Jake put his chin on the table.

"Nobody'll ever believe us," he said, "so I don't think we should tell anybody."

"I agree."

They heard their father's truck in the driveway.

"Daddy's home," Livy said.

"We're not telling him."

"I know."

They heard his door slam.

"Jake?!" he cried.

They could barely hear him.

Jake slid his chair back, jumped up, and headed for the driveway.

When he reached his father, Dr. James was standing beside the truck wearing his head-to-toe green camou-flage outfit, grinning like a boy, and holding upside down a huge turkey gobbler. It's wings hung wide and outspread, almost touching the ground.

"What do you think?" he said.

"Wow!" Jake cried.

"Yes! That's what I thought! Listen, Jake—this is the high point of my turkey-hunting career so far—I called him all the way across the river! Can you imagine that?"

"No, sir. How far away was he?"

"Son, he started out nearly a mile off! I gave a few yelps—my sweet little hen call, you know—and right away I had that sucker excited. Well, I held off. I was hunkered down in my blind—in that spot I found—anyhow, I waited and *finally* I let him have another whisper."

He dropped the heavy turkey to the gravel and snatched the box call from his pocket.

"Just like this," he said.

He made a few sharp, soft yelps.

"A sweeter sound no courting gobbler ever heard," he said.

"No, sir, I guess not."

"Well, he made his appearance on the river bank. I could just see him from my spot; his blue-black feathers were reflecting that sunlight like oil, or armor—oh, I don't know what all. But he was a sight, let me tell you."

"I know he was."

"I let him sweat. If you want this pretty lady, I said to myself, come on over and get her."

He grinned and Jake hoped he could someday feel this happy about something.

"Two little tiny yelps, barely audible, and I put the caller down in the leaves. I said to myself, the worst mistake you can make is calling too much."

"Yes, sir."

"Okay, then I just settled in to wait. Finally, he

couldn't stand it! Gobbled one time, and lifted himself into the air on those black wings, and sailed right to me."

"He landed near your blind?"

"Right in front. I had my twelve gauge up already; all I had to do was lean out behind a little sapling, and blow his head off."

"Gee," Jake said, looking at the great bird that, indeed, had a neck but no head.

The man put his big arm around his son's shoulders. "It was quick."

"Yes, sir," Jake said with a swallow.

"I know you don't care for killing, Jake boy."

Jake was silent, gazing at the bird, wishing with all his heart he could tell his father what was going on.

"Rather buy 'em at the supermarket, wouldn't you, eh? But son . . ." he assumed a warm, confidential tone ". . . there's more to this hunting. It's not something everybody can do, you know? There's a craft involved, and patience to endure the cold, or the mosquitoes . . . It takes guts, boy, old-fashioned courage . . ."

"Yes, sir."

"And beyond that, when you take a deer's life, or a big old turkey gobbler's, it *means* something, son. It takes you right out of this ordinary world. All of a sudden you understand the other men who've done it; you speak their language, you belong in their club. Aw, Jake, I can't really explain it. You just have to experience it to know what I mean."

"I guess," Jake said. He wasn't sure about all this; but

the one thing he knew was that he couldn't begin to talk about what really mattered to him.

"When you pass through that gate," his father concluded grandly, "it sure does get in your blood."

I could tell you about passing through gates, Jake thought.

Livy came around the truck.

"Ohhh!" she said, seeing the turkey.

"Just think about the dressing and cranberry sauce, honey," her father said with a grin.

He was in a hurry to get back to the hospital, so he rushed off to the shower. A gardener was supposed to clean the bird.

Jake walked rapidly to the tunnel door, and Livy followed him.

"What are you doing?" she asked. "Did you tell him anything?"

"What's the use? Daddy doesn't know what's going on. Any more than Granny. Nobody does!" he cried as he kicked the weathered door.

"I do," Livy said gently, touching his arm.

"Yeah."

He stood there, staring at the old silvery boards, trying to forgive his father and mother for being in their own worlds.

"What gets me," Jake said, "is Daddy talking that way about guts. I wonder if he'd go in there."

Livy stood still beside him a long time without talking, hoping she could comfort him somehow.

"I guess Darcy's destroyed by now," Jake finally said in a low voice.

She nodded.

"At least Colonel Ruffin didn't get out—that's one thing to be glad about."

"It sure is."

"You wouldn't see him if he did," a woman's voice said.

They spun around and faced Sarantha.

"We wouldn't?" Jake asked angrily. "Why not?"

"Lands, no! Ghosts be invisible when they wants to!" She smiled and used a charming voice, as if nothing were wrong.

"Well? Did he escape then?"

"Not so far," Sarantha said softly, becoming sad.

"You tricked us," Jake said, taking a step toward her and then, thinking better, stepping back.

"I'm sorry," she whispered, sniffling.

"You lied," Livy said.

"It was jus' fo' little Darcy," Sarantha said guiltily. "She my baby. You mighta done it, in my place."

"I liked her," Livy said.

Sarantha broke into tears at this, crying into the back of her hand.

"Is the below-world gone?" Jake asked loudly.

"Not quite, not quite," she sniffled, "but it about to be, sho' is."

Jake grabbed the cave door and pulled it open.

"Stop!" Livy cried. "Tell him he can't!" she said to Sarantha.

"You better not," Sarantha said weakly.

"Tell him!" Livy yelled at her.

"My Darcy," Sarantha said, sobbing away.

"Jake, no!" Livy screamed.

"It's my life," he said, looking into the darkness.

All he could think of was Daddy, standing in the driveway and telling him about courage.

"Oh, child," Sarantha said. "I jus' don't know how to thank you."

"Shut up!" Livy screamed at her. "Just shut up!"

Jake disappeared inside.

"I'm getting Granny," Livy said, taking off at a run.

CHAPTER TEN

In a Dying World

Livy found Granny with a new touring group. Yanking
crinkly ruffles to get her attention, she blurted out that
Jake was in the tunnel of ghosts. The ladies thought it
was a play of some kind, a form of antebellum entertainment. But they quieted down when Granny shoved
Livy, sending her into a delicate maple rocker.

"I didn't mean to push you so hard, dear," Granny
said, adjusting her skirts, "but you have *got* to learn to
be truthful!"

Livy rolled over once and got up, no longer shouting,
and ran from the room.

She stopped in the toolshed long enough to grab the
spotlight, then kept going. When she reached the tunnel
door, Sarantha was up against the wall, covering her face
and crying. Another figure towered over her. He was
black, too, with angry eyes and a powerful feeling about
him.

"I am The Keeper," he said in a deep, calm voice, "and I have come to punish Sarantha."

"What about Jake?" Livy snapped.

"Your brother is a brave boy. By this undertaking, he will make rapid progress on the soul's path. He may even skip several lifetimes."

"I mean what about him right now?" Livy cried.

"He is gone. This one tricked him."

"He's gone?"

"Passed through the timegate."

"I begged him not to go," Sarantha sobbed.

"You pretended to beg!" The Keeper thundered.

Livy stepped back from him.

"You sealed your fate," The Keeper continued, "when you locked them inside."

"That was you?" Livy asked.

"I jus' wanted my baby back!"

"How could you?" Livy said, her voice rising.

Sarantha hid her face and cried.

"Well, I want my brother back!"

"I'm sorry, child," The Keeper said.

"Is he still alive?" she snapped.

"Yes, but only for a little longer. He's going to sacrifice everything for a world not his own. You see, it may be hard for you to understand . . . here in the above-world his father is blind to his courage; Dr. James continues to invite him to the rituals of his own time, paying no attention to the real passages of Jake's life."

"Words, words, words!" Livy screamed, running past him into the cave. These ghosts! she thought, heading down the path, first they trick you, then they stand around talking when you need them!

She crossed the cave-in point and scanned the ground for Jake's footprints. Where they disappeared would be the timegate. And she saw the spot.

She stopped before it for a moment.

And took deep breaths.

And took a giant step.

Again she felt herself flying effortlessly down a long, dark, cool space.

Then it was hot and bright all around her, and there was a roar like a loud rushing railroad train.

Fires fanned and leapt all over the pasture. Its grass was scorched brown now, and she was looking right at a tornado, bending and curving as it roared across the field. A crack in the earth before her began to widen with a slow, powerful noise.

"Arrrgghhh!"

It was a human cry against the winds and crackling fires, and she spotted the form of the colonel across the opening in the earth. He was still on his horse, and it was rearing up with wild eyes. Colonel Ruffin looked just as frightened and crazy, and he was waving his sword over his head.

"I see you! I see you!" he yelled.

Now he knows the spot, Livy thought. He's been here looking for it up to the very last.

An earthquake shook the world and rattled Livy and the colonel's horse to the ground. Where is Jake? she thought, staring into the widening abyss.

She turned around, and there was a narrow land

bridge between crevasses, leading off toward the distant woods.

Quickly, she ran down it, heading in the general direction of the mansion, and getting away from the colonel. Against the noises of destruction she could barely hear him cursing.

When she ran fast her feet crunched down into the earth, and she realized its crust was crumbling like everything else. But she kept on, praying Jake was ahead of her. The sky was a strange silver-and-peach color, like a hot sunset coming down to smother the pasture.

She came to the woods and ran into the trees, even though there were bursts of white light ahead, as if giant flashbulbs were shooting off. She found the path to the house and took it, and as she passed an ancient oak it swelled up and exploded beside her. The hot blast knocked her over, and she saw blue-and-white light streaming from the crater of its stump, as glowing red chunks of wood passed over her head.

It was hard to breathe as she ran on, galloping now and sucking in all the dry air she could swallow. Her feet went down to her ankles with each step, and the temperature kept rising.

When she broke into the open gardens of the big house she saw Jake pulling on the knob of the basement door.

"Jake! Jake!" she screamed.

Hot winds twisted the magnolias around like saplings, and drowned her voice in the sound.

"Jake!" she cried, running close to him.

"No!" he said. "You weren't supposed to come!"

"I couldn't leave you! Where's Darcy?"

"Don't know yet. This door is bolted from the inside. Come on!"

They ran up the stairs to the gallery. Jake picked up two pieces of stove wood from the stack there and crashed them through the French windows.

Livy followed him into the jagged opening and they hurried down the inside steps; Jake unbolted the basement door.

Something moved in the darkness, and Jake took a burning oil lantern down from its wall hook; its light spread against the dusty walls.

A few steps within and they saw a long row of huge cages.

"Jake!" Livy said, clutching his sleeve.

They took another step.

Shadowy forms emerged from the backs of the cells, human forms, bony and sad and ragged, clutching the bars and glaring out with sunken eyes.

"Who are you?" Jake cried.

"We souls," one of them said.

"We used to be slaves, an' now we still slaves," another said with a rusty, unused voice. "Who are you?"

"They the ones!" the first voice cried.

"What ones?" Jake asked.

"The ones come to save us!"

"Jake? Jake and Livy?"

It was Darcy's voice from far down the wall.

They ran to her as another spirit yelled, "Hallelujah!" Arms reached out hard, and clawed in the air for them.

Jake rattled the bars of Darcy's cage. They were almost too hot to touch but they didn't crumble.

"Where are the keys?" he screamed.

"We don't know! We don't know!"

"Please save us!"

Over the moaning and yelling they heard a thunderous crash.

"The roof! The roof!" Darcy cried. "We ain't got no time!"

"Where are the keys?!" Jake pleaded.

"Don't nobody know!" Darcy said. "Thas all we been talkin' 'bout in here!"

Livy grabbed Jake's arm.

"William might know!" she said. "He's the one who might know!"

"Come on!" he said.

They went out the backyard door, with the caged slaves crying and begging them not to go.

They ran through the burned-up garden as the magnolia tops burst into flame high above their heads.

As they crashed up the brick walk to William's cottage their legs sank to their knees in the fragile crust.

Jake easily pushed William's door open.

He was tied to his bed, with a gag around his mouth, and Jake grabbed a butcher knife from the wall beside the stove and began to cut him free.

"Y'all come back," William said, coughing. "I don't believe it."

"Where are the keys to the cages?" Livy said.

"I sho' didn't believe y'all would."

"The keys, William! The keys!"

"Colonel Ruffin, after all I done fo' him, he said if he couldn't make it out of here, then neither was nobody else."

"Do you have the keys?" Livy screamed.

"Sho' do," he said, pointing his long finger toward a nail in the wall.

An iron ring hung from it, strung with heavy keys.

Jake grabbed the ring and burned his fingers. He wrapped it in his shirttail, took William's hand and led them from the cottage.

They were sinking a little deeper in the earth now, and were forced to slow down and take careful steps.

Burning pieces of the magnolias fell streaming into the garden as they worked through it, and darkening layers of smoke hung before them on the heavy air.

William seemed dazed, and he kept mumbling about how the colonel had tied him.

They went through the basement door and heard the choking coughing of the slaves. The house was raging with fire above them, and blisters were popping out on the huge ceiling beams.

Jake felt his hands searing as he worked the ring of keys in the ancient locks, and as each rusty cell door opened, Livy and William pulled the smoke-filled souls inside to their feet. Finally Jake came to Darcy's cell, and he couldn't get a key to fit. The heat was unbearable now, and there was no more air to breathe.

"Help me!" Darcy screamed in a hoarse whisper.

Jake grabbed the scorching hot bars of the cell door and ripped it from its hinges.

Then Jake and Livy and William and Darcy and all

the others ran from the burning mansion, dodged through the edge of the garden and ran into the woods as the house collapsed upon itself in a dragon's roar of flame.

They found the path and ran between exploding trees. Now and then one of them would fall through the earth's crust to his waist, and have to be pulled up by the others. Red coals flew from the fiery trunks and burned their arms.

Jake began to lose hope because he couldn't breathe. But something kept him going, leading the others in a chain of locked hands, one foot at a time in the treacherous crust as the trees burst in blinding white blasts all around. He hardly believed it when he was finally standing at the great pasture's edge and staring out on an unfamiliar wasteland of canyons and ledges, fire tongues licking from the cracks, smoke and steam feeding up into the layer of black that hung in the air beneath the reddening sky.

"Come this way!" Livy cried, taking the lead, and she showed them the land bridge she had crossed on. Now it was only a foot wide, and the thin column of dirt and rock that supported it was moving and trembling, slowly seeking a new position. But it was the only way left to the timegate.

They started out upon it, feet sideways to each abyss, trying not to look down.

"Hey! Hey over there!"

It was the colonel, still separated from the timegate. His horse was gone now, but he stood and slashed the air with his saber.

"You can't do that! You can't get out of here!" he yelled.

Jake saw that the colonel's thin shelf of footing was gradually moving toward theirs, rejoining, and easing him toward the gate, too.

"Faster," Jake said, looking over his shoulder.

Darcy was last in line, and she was falling behind the others.

"Come on, Darcy!" Jake screamed. "If we can do it you can, too!"

"Yeah!" Livy cried. "Come on, girl!"

"I'll see you all in hell first!" Colonel Ruffin yelled, cutting up the layer of fiery mist before him.

Then Jake was beside the timegate.

There came a creaking deep in the earth, and the colonel's thin shelf of footing moved toward them a little faster.

"Hurry!" Jake said, letting William go through the timegate first.

William disappeared from sight.

"All right!" Jake yelled in his raw throat.

Then one by one the spirits from the cages passed by Jake with their suffering eyes, and vanished in the gate through time.

"I can't! I can't!" Darcy screamed, and Livy was moving back along the shelf of land toward her.

"No, Livy! No!" Jake yelled. "She can do it on her own! Don't go back, she'll pull you over!"

But Livy kept moving at a steady rate and staring into Darcy's eyes, carefully avoiding the great holes on either side of her. Tips of orange flames appeared out of both cracks, and the sky was a wet varnished red—as if a bloody, glowing sun had melted all across it—and it pulsed with brighter and brighter light.

Now Livy held Darcy's hand, and pulled her without a word.

The colonel's ledge was no more than ten feet from Jake's, and he was calmer, Jake saw, grinning and watching and waiting.

"I've been in tighter spots than this!" the colonel cried, his eyes gleaming with success.

"You'll never make it!" Jake yelled.

The colonel trembled and almost fell.

"You're the one who'll die in this world!" Colonel Ruffin screamed. "You and all who scheme and plan to destroy our way of life!"

"Your way of life stinks!" Jake yelled.

The colonel slashed his blade at Jake.

"Come *on,* Darcy!" Livy said, pulling her close to Jake.

"Get through here!" Jake said.

Livy squeezed past Jake holding Darcy's hand.

"Hurry!" Livy said to Jake, as she and Darcy vanished through the gate.

Now the colonel was no more than six feet away. Jake saw every line in his weathered face, every hair of his long blond military moustache, and the bright determination in his cold blue eyes. Behind him the red lacquered sky met the burning line of trees, and the land itself became a sheet of liquid flame, flowing toward them, pulling up the fires in the earthquake cracks as it came.

Colonel Ruffin crouched for a leap, his tongue crossed

his lips once, and he smiled as he sprang through the air.

Jake dodged into the timegate, and felt himself sucked weightless into darkness and the cool, free motion of flight, hurtling down a long and burdenless space.

He couldn't tell whether the colonel was behind him.

CHAPTER ELEVEN

Celebrating Spirits

When Jake finally found himself staggering in the cave beneath his house, it was as brightly lit as the garden at noon. Blinking into the lights, he realized there were faces in the glare.

"Jake, boy!" his father cried, rushing to hug him.

"Daddy?" he said, dazed.

"Right here, son," he said, squeezing Jake.

Jake saw Livy in Mom's arms, and Granny standing by.

"Where's Darcy?" he asked Livy.

"I never saw her after we came through."

"How long have you been here?" Jake asked his father.

"Not long; we came down on Granny's say-so. Livy stirred her up and she investigated, and found the tunnel door open."

Granny beamed.

"Naturally she called us right away—once she saw

Livy's and your footprints disappearing inside this place!" his father said.

Jake shaded his eyes with his hand and looked closely at his father.

"What happened next?" Jake asked urgently. "It's important."

"I came in with a flashlight, and followed your tracks until they ran out, right there." He pointed to the time-gate spot.

"But you didn't touch it?" Jake said.

"No, son, almost did . . . but I was standing here staring down at the end of your trail, trying to figure out where you went, and by chance I kicked a little rock with my toe. It rolled over there and just flat vanished; beat all I ever saw."

"Through the timegate," Jake said.

"So Livy told us. Son, you two have stumbled onto something mightly strange in this place."

Jake wanted to laugh, but he was so tired, so glad to see the family and so worried about the colonel, that he couldn't.

"What did you do next? I've got to know exactly what you saw."

"Well, I tossed in some more rocks, not believing what I was seeing. I started thinking of black holes in space, crazy stuff like that. Then I ran back for your mom and we brought her photography lights." He swept his arm toward the glare.

"Then what?" Jake asked impatiently.

"We got here and waited a few minutes, threw in a lot of pebbles . . . Kept doing it, just reminding ourselves we were on to something totally new, totally un-known. Well, my patience was wearing thin; I'd about decided to take a step and find out for myself what hap-pened to you, and all of a sudden here comes this weird light, sort of a purplish flickering smokelike shape. It popped into the tunnel and floated right past us."

"It nearly touched me," Granny said.

"A whole batch of them came through," their father said, "almost seeming like they were alive."

"I told you they were," Livy said quietly.

"One of them passed right through my arm," Granny said. "I think."

"Then what?" Jake said.

"Well, here comes your sister, pretty as the day she was born. She appeared out of nowhere just like you did, only she had one of those purple light things flow-ing out of her hand."

"Darcy," Jake said, glancing at Livy. She nodded.

"Daddy," he said, "this is real important now. Did you see one of those things with me? Or right behind me?"

"Sure didn't. Why?"

"Mom? Granny? Did you?" Jake asked.

"No," his mother said. She had been crying.

"Let me think," Granny said, trying to decide.

"Did you or not?" Livy asked angrily.

"I believe not," Granny said, offended.

Jake and Livy sighed.

"I guess he didn't make it," Jake said.

"Who?" his father asked. "And what on earth is this thing you're so worried about?"

"Just a minute."

Jake reached down for a small pebble and tossed it toward the timegate. Instead of vanishing, it hit the dirt and bounced.

"It's gone!" Livy cried.

"Looks that way. No more below-world."

He tried pebbles a few more times, and none of them disappeared.

"Any time you're ready to talk," his father said, "we're ready to listen."

Jake stared at him for a moment.

"Daddy," he began, "Livy and I have been in a place called the below-world with spirits of slaves, and the spirit, or ghost, of their master. He was Colonel Ruffin, who used to own Tapalyla Hill."

"Now wait a minute," Granny said, indignant.

"Hush, Mother," their mother said.

"But the children are desecrating Mrs. Ruffin's legend, can't you see that?"

"You saw the stones disappear," their mother said, annoyed.

"Not any more they don't!" Granny cried triumphantly, as if that fact disposed of the story.

Their father turned to her in fury. "Did you see these children appear before your very eyes?"

"Well, well . . ." Granny glanced nervously about the cave.

"Certainly you did!" her son-in-law thundered. "Don't you think they deserve a hearing?"

Granny began humming to herself, as if her mind were entirely elsewhere.

"We'll tell you later how all this came about," Jake said to his father. "But right now I think we should check on our attic."

"The attic?" his mother asked.

"Yes. It's been full of evil spirits, brought here by the Old Confederacy Celebration. And if the colonel's ghost did get through, that's where he'll be."

"Yeah," Livy said. "But if he is there, what can we do about it now?"

"I don't know," Jake said. "Maybe The Keeper can help, maybe Sarantha can. Anyway, I don't want that old rat in my attic, and I'll bet I can run him out."

Their parents took each other's hands, squeezing tight and seeming worried. Jake realized this was a strange sight, their being so close, on the same side, and his father unsure of himself.

"Son," he said, "tell us one thing now. Why did the Celebration attract evil ghosts?"

"Because of slavery," Jake said. "All this excitement . . . especially in our house . . . Can we go check the attic now?"

"By all means," their father mumbled, following his son out of the cave.

The family emerged into the garden at sundown. The sky was streaked with dark grays and pale lavenders, and the roof line stood out strongly. Jake stopped and watched it, the others gathering behind him, and, just as he hoped, a flicker of purple drifted from the shingles like smoke, a shape-shifting form that glowed dimly from within, and it seemed to float aimless and distracted into the night sky.

Another and another followed, each drifting in a different direction.

"They're going!" Jake whispered, grabbing Livy's hand.

Jake and Livy felt the family gathering closely around them, touching their shoulders, watching silently as the unhappy spirits floated free of the old house.

"They realize Colonel Ruffin isn't coming," Livy said.

"Yes," Jake said, "the others must have told them."

"What others?" their mother asked.

"Oh, some ghosts of slaves that we freed."

"You freed slaves?" Granny asked, the blood draining from her face.

"The reason those evil ones are leaving," Jake said, pointing to the roof and ignoring Granny, "is because they know this house isn't good for them anymore . . . There's not enough of the spirit they need."

"This is the most ridiculous thing I ever heard," Granny said. "You children have gone wild. You've become mad dogs, frothing at the mouth."

"*Hush*, Mother!" her daughter said.

Granny stared at her with ferocious blue eyes, which seemed to catch the final moments of sunset light. She wasn't used to being reprimanded.

They stood there as the last of the vaporous spirits wafted into the night sky.

"Let's go inside," their father said in a quiet voice.

They did, and he led them to the big stone fireplace in the living room. Their mother went to the kitchen to make a pot of tea while he laid a fire of white oak logs.

"*You* want a fire?" Livy asked.

"I believe it's cold enough, don't you?"

"Oh, sure . . . I guess so. It's just that you never want one."

"I don't do everything right," he said.

Jake and Livy had never heard him say anything like that before.

When they all were comfortable with their tea, Jake and Livy began to tell the whole story from the time of the attic knockings and Sarantha's voice saving Jake from bees. Their father sat listening so silently, in such amazement, that he never even lifted his cup.

"You know," he said, "I have to keep remembering those stones—the way they disappeared into nowhere—to take all this in."

"How do you think we feel?" Livy said, smiling. "All along we kept expecting to wake up from a dream or something."

"The thing is," their father said slowly, staring at the fire, "what you have discovered . . . it calls for such great changes in the way we think. Scientifically . . . religiously . . ."

During this conversation Granny had disappeared into the house. Now she entered the living room with an artificial smile.

"Listening to this is all well and good," she said, "but it is past time to get ready for the ball."

"The ball," their father said.

"Yes, indeed! You haven't forgotten you are the general this year!"

"It's strange," he said, "but a few hours ago I was dwelling on the irony of it all—I finally get chosen

General of the Ball, and that year my wife refuses to go with me."

"I didn't want to hurt you, but—" she began.

"No, no—you were quite right about it . . . I see that now."

"We don't want to be late!" Granny said in a shrill voice, pretending the conversation wasn't happening.

Their father sat back in his deep leather chair and looked at the children calmly. "If what you believe is true," he said, "then the Old Confederacy Celebration, and especially the ball, contributes to this evil-spirit business, right?"

"That's what we understand," Jake said evenly.

His father looked at Granny. "They can forget it," he said.

"You don't mean you'd back out now?"

"You heard me, unless you've lost your hearing altogether."

"You owe it to them!" Granny cried. "They'll think you've died!"

Her son-in-law put his big hand over his mouth and gazed at the fire.

"You have a point there," he said.

"Of course they would! Why, Maynard, tonight is the very peak of honor for you; how can you even *think* of not attending?"

"Go get ready," he snapped.

Granny straightened her neck and hurried away.

"You're going to do it?" his wife asked wearily.

"Not precisely what she thinks." He was smiling and

his eyes were dancing with a plan. "I have an idea . . . If only they won't mind . . ."

"Who?" his wife asked as he got up.

"Tell you in a minute," he said, heading for the kitchen.

They heard him dialing the telephone.

Their mother reached out and took each of her children by the hand.

"Whatever happened down there, I'm so glad you're back."

"Me, too," Livy said.

"And I'm awfully proud of you."

"Why?" Jake asked.

"Because you were both so brave, trying to help that little girl. And you stood up to the colonel. But don't you *ever* go down there again, you hear me?"

"I know I won't," Livy said with a tired smile.

"Me either," Jake said. "But I do hope Sarantha appears to us one more time, and tells us what happened."

His father came back into the room grinning.

"I'm in luck," he said. "You know I have a good many black patients, but did you know three of them are choir directors in their churches?"

"No, sir," Jake said.

"They sure are. With the most fantastic choirs you ever heard, too. I've seen 'em on local TV, early Sunday morning."

"What on earth are you doing, Maynard?" his wife asked.

"A little surprise for the ball," he said. "Now let's hurry, if you can all still find your outfits."

Jake and Livy looked at their mother. They were invited because Daddy was the general and they had agreed not to go, but clearly things were now changed, somehow.

They headed off to their bedrooms.

Soon the whole family was dressed up and in the car, driving to the Celebration Ball. Daddy wore his tuxedo, and Granny's stiff blue finger-curls were bouncing.

"What an honor," she said. "General of the Ball."

"Yes, indeed," her son-in-law replied.

Jake considered Granny as they rode. He hadn't really expected anything from her, but because his father had taken the day's events so seriously her indifference suddenly stood out. In fact, she seemed to be beyond the power of responding to all that had happened with the slavery ghosts, as if she were simply too young to comprehend it. *That makes her about three or four,* he thought.

They reached the hall and their father parked. Granny walked a little ahead of the rest of them, and charged eagerly through the crowded doorway.

Inside, everyone was festive, sipping drinks and slapping Dr. James on the back if they could reach him. There were beautiful Confederate-style dresses of taffeta and velvet edged with eyelet embroidery and lace, some of calico and dotted swiss with ribbons, all puffed wide by wire rims and layers of starched crinoline petticoats. But no one outdid Granny's handmade pride, a hot pink gown of silk organza.

After a few moments of polite grinning and hand-shaking, their mother and Livy and Jake escaped upstairs to the dark balcony overlooking the party. Well-tailored servants, the only black people in the hall, moved among the guests carrying trays of drinks. The band struck up "Magnolias Under the Moonlight," and everyone except Granny was dancing and drinking away. She didn't drink at all and disapproved of it, but she loved the once-yearly spectacle, with all the wealthiest folk in town gossiping around her. She could pick up more talk on one ball night than in six months of Sundays.

Finally it was time for the formal presentation of this year's general, and of the young girl who had been chosen as his lady.

"If you ever play that role," her mother said in Livy's ear, "I'll skin you alive."

Livy giggled tiredly and leaned against her mother's arm.

The wooden seats grew hard. Jake was exhausted, and he wished his father would hurry up with whatever surprise he had planned.

Finally it was time for drunken speeches about the Old South, and the raising of toasts to her gallant culture so nobly preserved by the members of the ball.

Jake wondered whether any of the evil ghosts had come here.

Then, for the grand finale of the ceremony, the band played "Dixie," and everyone leapt into chorus on the first bar:

"Away down South where I was born, early on a frosty morn, look away, look away, look away, Dixieland. In Dix-

ieland I'll take my stand, to live and die in Dixie, hooray, hooray, away down South .... in Dixie!"

There was screaming and clapping, rebel-yelling and crying, backslapping, hand-squeezing and the hugging of brothers and sisters in Confederate lore and modern wealth.

Then Jake and Livy's father stepped up to the microphone and said, "Good people? I'd like just one more word."

He must have cranked the volume up, because his voice was so loud it immediately hushed the din.

"Folks," he said, "we've been coming here for years and years to celebrate the Old South . . ."

There was clapping all around. A drunk yelled, "Amen, doc!"

"But tonight I've got a little surprise for you. I thought at first I might try explaining something—'course, I know how you love long speeches . . ."

There was laughter and mild booing.

"So I thought I'd make my point another way. I've invited a few friends to join us here at the ball, and I believe they're just coming in the doorway now."

A gasping noise rolled across the crowd, and they fell absolutely silent, staring at the entrances filling with people, black people, dozens and then scores of men in white shirts and black ties and women in silky, organdy dresses, all wearing the most solemn and serious expressions. They made their way down to the center of the dance floor by the band.

"Band leader," Dr. James boomed over the mike, "give us an *A*."

The musicians complied, and a hum began among the newcomers, a growing steady humming with overtones and harmonies; it was like some incredible human instrument warming up, or checking its tuning. Jake thought of the moment before an orchestra begins.

And then the voices sang, *"Amazing grace, how sweet the sound, that saved a wretch like me. I once was lost, but now I'm found, was blind, but now I see."*

Their mother put her arms through Jake's and Livy's. "It's beautiful," she whispered.

Jake nodded. But Livy asked, "Will everybody be mad at Daddy?"

"I don't know," her mother said.

The choir sang on, its power and richness increasing with each verse.

"Through many dangers, toils and snares, I have already come; 'tis grace hath bro't me safe thus far, and grace will lead me home."

Jake turned to his mother and her face was wet with tears. "I'm so proud of him," she whispered.

"But will they get the point?" Jake asked. "These people might think it's some kind of entertainment."

"Maybe—but look how they've taken over the drunken atmosphere, and made it spiritual."

"I'll bet the bad ghosts are flying through the roof," Livy said.

"When we've been there ten thousand years," the choir sang, *"bright shining as the sun, we've no less days, to sing God's praise, than when we'd first begun. Amazing grace, how sweet the sound, that saved a wretch like me, I once was lost, but now I'm found, was blind, but now I see. Amen."*

There was silence over the hall.

Then the black women and men began to turn, and to slip back to the doors through which they had come.

When they had all left, and the partyers were standing hushed and stunned, Jake and Livy's father grabbed the mike one last time.

"Thank you very much, folks," he said gently, "and good night."

He made for the front door, and not one of his friends spoke to him as he walked among them.

Jake and Livy and their mother hurried from the balcony and met him at the car. There was no Granny in sight.

"I guess she'll find herself a ride home," their father said.

"I believe that's the idea," his wife replied with a smile.

CHAPTER TWELVE

Ghostly Goodbyes

Jake and Livy didn't talk all the way home, they just rode along in the back seat thinking of what their father had done. Jake admired and appreciated it, but on the other hand it was what his father himself would have called grandstanding, or showboating—and in a way, it was stealing Jake's and Livy's thunder. But it doesn't matter, Jake thought. That's the nice thing about what we went through—you realize how much doesn't matter. That's Daddy's way of doing everything, being right at the center. But what will happen to him now? Will his friends turn on him, and his patients leave his practice?

The car wheeled into the driveway and came to a stop.

Their parents started into the house, but Jake touched Livy's arm and stopped her.

"We'll be just a few minutes," he said.

"What now?" his mother said, smiling.

"Don't worry. I want to see if we can contact Sarantha and Darcy again."

His parents looked at each other.

"Ask them if they'll talk with me," his father said, grinning as he followed his wife into the house.

Jake and Livy hurried to the spot beneath the magnolia where they had first seen Sarantha. It was a chilly spring night, with the stars twinkling through thick leaves here and there.

"I'm glad *this* garden isn't burned up," Livy said.

"Yeah, me too."

"Do you think they'll come?"

Jake shrugged his shoulders.

"Greetings, Jake," a deep voice said.

He jumped and turned. The Keeper's form was just emerging.

"Hello," Jake said.

"You have done well," The Keeper said. "If you continue this way, you will be able to skip several lifetimes of struggle."

"You mean there's more of this coming?" Jake asked.

"Not exactly. What I meant was, you have already progressed greatly on the task you set yourself in this life."

"And what is that?"

"Surely you know. Think for a moment."

Jake was sure it had something to do with courage—with having guts—but he didn't want to say it. He realized suddenly that he hadn't worried about his bravery since the below-world time.

"That's right," The Keeper said.

"You can read minds, too?" Jake asked.

"Only when you allow it," The Keeper said. "You have your privacy when you really want it."

"What will happen to Sarantha?" Livy asked.

"She has been severely warned. Part of her punishment is the guilt she now feels at having risked your safety."

Two forms materialized in the air beside them.

It was Sarantha and Darcy, with smiling teary faces and their arms around each other.

"I'm so sorry, y'all," Sarantha said.

"Well, you got her back," Livy said calmly. "That's what you wanted."

"It sho' was. An' I'm gon' be grateful to you an' Jake fo'ever an' ever."

Jake was still a little angry with Sarantha, but he was glad Darcy had gotten out of the below-world in time. And he knew it never would have happened without Sarantha's tricks.

"What happens to you now?" Jake asked Darcy. "Will you have to begin another contract with Colonel Ruffin, to work out all the trouble left between you?"

"Y'all ain't heard?" Darcy said joyfully. "When he grabbed me up that time, an' you got through the gate, he was fixin' to lock me up in the cages. But I slipped out a' his arms an' ran like a devil, an' hid out in the woods."

"But you were in a cage when we found you," Livy said.

"Thas 'cause I tried my rescue! I went in there an' did the bes' I could to get them folks out! Colonel Ruffin,

he come an' caught me an' all, but it don't matter—
'cause I tried! I done my bes' an' now he ain't got nothin'
to do with me."

"That's great," Livy said.

"It sho' is." Darcy grinned.

"At least something was accomplished," Jake said. "But
what about the colonel? What happens to him now?"

"He will experience the fires of destruction for a while
longer," The Keeper said, "and then be reborn as a slave,
in a new place like the below-world."

"Hooray!" Darcy and Livy cried. The Keeper frowned
at them.

"Colonel Ruffin actually agreed to this contract?" Jake
asked.

"His higher self did."

"It's hard to believe he has one," Livy said.

"Not so, child," The Keeper replied. "The colonel's
greater self knows he must experience slavery before he
can fully grasp what he's been doing and repent."

"Darcy an' I got to go now," Sarantha said. "Thanks
so much again!"

"Wait, Sarantha!" Livy cried. But they vanished.

The Keeper glared at the space where they had been.

"She has much to learn," he grumbled.

"Keeper," Livy said, "Jake seems to know what his
task is, but what about mine? Do I have one, too?"

"Look within yourself for a moment. What is the thing
you would *most* like to change?"

"Well . . . sometimes I get so mad at Granny . . .
and I wonder if I'm not a little mean to her . . ."

"Excellent."

"You mean that's it? I'm mean?"

"No, child. You are impatient. You see, you have the gift of sharp intelligence, and a quick response to people. You must learn to discipline it—not to hurt others with it."

"Granny says she could slice through stove wood with that tongue of hers," Jake said.

"This is her business," The Keeper said ominously.

"Yes, sir."

Then The Keeper turned back to Livy, and seemed gentler.

"You and your grandmother have entered into a contract, too, remember."

"You mean I have a contract with everybody I know?"

"All you are close to."

"But what's Granny's part of it?" Livy asked.

"Ah, me," The Keeper said, sighing deeply, "poor Granny."

"What do you mean?" Jake asked, smiling.

"I've told you all I can," The Keeper said. "Most people live their whole lives without this much information about their plan."

"Most people don't go into the below-world," Jake said.

The Keeper began to fade.

"Wait!" Livy cried. "We've got lots more questions!"

"Search within," The Keeper said from a distance.

"Please stay a little longer," Jake said.

And from a far away place, invisible through the space where he had been, in a very formal voice, The Keeper said one last word.

"Seek."

Jake and Livy stood there in silence.

"Nobody would ever believe us," she said at last.

"I know it."

"At least Mom and Daddy did."

"Yeah. I still can't get over that. He really seems different now."

"Shall we tell him about The Keeper?"

"Sure."

They walked slowly to the house.

When they reached the sun room, their mother was hanging up the phone.

"You won't believe this," she said. "Five calls have already come in, saying how precious it was of Maynard to arrange that little 'display' at the ball!"

"Display?" Jake said.

"That's what they think it was! It seems that they've all talked it over, and decided it was right in the spirit of the Old Confederacy Celebration—like having slaves come up from the quarters to sing!"

She was too exasperated to say any more.

"Fools!" Livy cried.

"They missed the whole point," Jake added. "They're as thick as Granny."

A car door slammed outside.

"Guess who's home," their mother said, rolling her eyes.

In a moment they heard the quick clicks of Granny's steps on the stairs, and she bustled into the room, her skirt and hooped petticoats springing through the tight doorway.

"Where's your daddy?" she said with a bright, demanding grin. "I've got to tell that man what a successful general he was!"

"Unfortunately," he said from the kitchen door, "I already know."

"My goodness," Granny said rapidly, "this is your finest hour. Everybody's saying they should have had the choir *years* ago! It adds such a touch to the whole thing!"

"Have you forgotten what your grandchildren did? What they *saw?*" he said angrily.

Granny looked at them, momentarily confused; then she grew fierce and tight, with the light of righteousness in her blue eyes.

"Those two are always making things up."

With that she turned and walked proudly from the room.

"Ohhhh," Livy said, squinting and shaking her fist after Granny.

"Now, now," Jake teased, "remember your task in this life."

"Yes, but—"

"No buts."

After a moment Livy smiled.

"Granny gives me lots of chances to practice, doesn't she?"

"She sure does, Livy, she sure does."

"What are you talking about?" their mother asked.

They explained about the contracts between people, and Livy's goal of learning patience.

"Well," their father said, "it seems there's more to life than we ever dreamed."

Their mother nodded.

There was a knock and Granny's head appeared in the door through which she had disappeared a moment before.

"Of course I don't expect any of you to believe me," she said, "but I have just seen the ghost of this house. I mean the *true* ghost, the original Mrs. Ruffin, and she is *exactly* as I have always imagined her to be!"

Everyone laughed, but her son-in-law got to his feet and said, "Let's have a look."

"She's gone now," Granny said. "Besides, she wouldn't show herself to people who tell stories!"

Granny hurried away, and the rest of the family laughed as quietly as they could, their hands over their mouths.

"In a way I can't blame her," their father said. "It's hard for me to believe, and I haven't spent my life serving this Old South thing the way she has."

His wife raised an eyebrow.

"Well, not the way *she* has!" he said, grabbing and hugging her.

Jake and Livy giggled. It was good to see their parents so relaxed together, and Jake had the feeling that in the days ahead all four of them would try together to understand what he and Livy had gone through.

But it didn't work out quite that way. The slavery ghosts became an uneasy secret shared by the family. The thumpings and appearances all stopped, and the tunnel door remained nailed shut, just a dusty reminder to the children. Their parents both found the spirit adventures too different and difficult to think about, and they seemed relieved when Jake and Livy stopped talking so much about them.

Granny was more than relieved, of course, and after a few claims of sighting Mrs. Ruffin, she let the whole business drop. Jake thought he noticed her being a little kinder to the gardener who still worked on the grounds of Tapalyla Hill, but he wasn't sure; he was positive, however, that his father treated him with more respect, and listened better. Their mother relaxed her campaign to teach the children the evils of Old South worship, and, once, she admitted a fear that her overdoing it had somehow brought on the bizarre happenings. As for Livy, she constantly tested her patience against Granny's tirades, and kept a score card in her room to measure progress.

Jake and Livy listened to the old house at night, just before sleep, following the cracking of a dry attic beam, or the quick run of a squirrel across the roof. Sometimes they sat on the low magnolia limb in the garden at dusk, hearing soft barred owls and doves, watching bullbats streak in the lavender sky and waiting for some hint from the other side.

They shared Granny's feeling that Tapalyla Hill was alive; to them it seemed linked with the busy spirit world, and they hoped someday to make another contact. But the weeks and months passed quietly, and the slavery ghosts spoke only in their dreams.

ALSO BY LUKE WALLIN

The Redneck Poacher's Son
Blue Wings